Roses Round The Door

DOREEN TOVEY

Roses Round The Door

Illustrated by Derek Crowe

MICHAEL JOSEPH · LONDON

First published in Great Britain by Michael Joseph Ltd
44 Bedford Square, London WC1
1982

ISBN 0 7181 2092 2

Photoset in Great Britain by
Alacrity Phototypesetters, Weston-super-Mare,
Printed by Hollen Street Press, Slough and
Bound by Hunter & Foulis, Edinburgh

Also by Doreen Tovey

CATS IN THE BELFRY

CATS IN MAY

DONKEY WORK

LIFE WITH GRANDMA

RAINING CATS AND DONKEYS

THE NEW BOY

DOUBLE TROUBLE

MAKING THE HORSE LAUGH

THE COMING OF SASKA

A COMFORT OF CATS

DEDICATION

For my husband René,
better known to readers as Charles,
without whose encouragement, enthusiasm
and exuberant enjoyment of life
I would never have written a single book.

Chapter One

I was ten years old when my Aunt Louisa took me to her friend Enna's wedding in the heart of the Somerset cider country — an event that was to have a considerable effect on my future life.

It probably had an effect on Louisa's, too. At twenty-three she was quite a stunner, even in the shiny beige stockings and strapped black patent shoes, the blue crêpe-de-chine dress with hip-length waist and the blue tulle Viking helmet with a splodge of silver leaves on the front that obscured her down to the eyebrows, like a chamber pot, and was the ultimate in fashionable bridesmaids' wear at the end of the twenties.

She was chief bridesmaid. The best man was a handsome young farmer called John, with Saxon blue eyes and hair as red-gold as the wheat that ripened in the fields that long-ago August Bank Holiday morning. He met us at the station with his pony and trap and pointed out his crops with his whip as we passed, and who knows what might have happened, it being the season of harvest and mellow fruitfulness and one wedding so often leading to another — at any rate it did in those days — if my grandmother hadn't seen to it that I went along to ensure that nothing did.

She didn't put it that way, of course. When Enna came to tea with us in Bristol a week before the wedding, my grandmother brought into the conversation the fact that I was motherless (my mother had died when I was born, my father was far away and Grandma, who was his mother, was bringing me up), mentioned in passing that I, too, would have liked to go to the wedding (actually it had never entered my mind: I'd rather have spent my time reading a True Western magazine borrowed from the boy next door any day than hang about at a soppy old wedding), and added, which *was* quite true, that I always went everywhere with Louisa (Grandma herself saw to that).

Before she knew where she was, Enna had said of course I must come, why hadn't she thought of it before, and would Grandma like to be a guest as well? My grandmother had assured her that she never went to weddings herself—it upset her too much, she said, seeing innocent young girls standing so trustingly at the altar not knowing what lay ahead of them—but it would be a nice day out for me. And so it was that a week later, wearing my best blue satin party dress topped with the prep school panama I insisted on wearing everywhere—I was an afficionado of *Schoolgirls' Own* as well as Westerns and, according to the illustrations, the girls of Morcove wore their school hats even when rescuing the French mistress from a cliff ledge or shadowing spies round the gym at midnight—there I was, experiencing the country at close quarters for the very first time, bowling along in a high-wheeled pony-trap between hedges garlanded with trails of late honeysuckle and ripening blackberries, past verges splashed with poppies as vivid as a Van Gogh painting and clumps of striking golden flowers that looked like stars.

I pointed them out to Louisa, who said they used those for harvest festival decoration. Thirteen years older than I was, she always adopted an omnipotent adult assurance about things where I was concerned.

'Ragwort thaat be. Kill a horse or cow stone dead if it gets into the haay." John corrected her in his slow West Country drawl. 'Nobody'd put thaat old stuff in the church. They do pull it up and burn it as soon as they do see it.'

Louisa blushed scarlet as a poppy herself with embarrassment. John, relenting, said, 'But what'd a young maid from town know about ragwort, though?' and moved closer to her. Seeing me regarding them with interest (at ten I took a beady-eyed interest in everything, particularly where Louisa and young men were concerned), he asked if I would like to drive the trap and handed me the reins. Topsy, he said, knew her way like a homing rook; he'd just take over at the end to make sure she stopped at the Martins' farm and not at the Dog and Duck. So we continued: John and Louisa looking at one another like Dante and Beatrice on the bridge in that picture by Henry Holiday, me driving the trap, panama at a rakish angle, pretending I was handling the Deadwood Stage — both occurrences guaranteed to give Grandma apoplexy had she known about them, but fortunately she was miles away in town. Peering happily over her glasses at the sock she was knitting for her brother William, most likely. Thinking how well, as usual, she'd managed everything.

She'd probably have dropped a stitch or two if she could have seen quite a few of the day's events. Most of them would have met with her approval, mind you. The ceremony itself, in the small square-towered Norman church set

against a background of bracken-covered hills. The homely congregation. The choir of earnest, apple-cheeked villagers with their eyes raised to heaven and black boots sticking out beneath their surplices. Enna herself, blushing modestly up the aisle in white satin. Grandma had her suspicions about girls who wore pink or blue. She said they usually had something on their consciences and time would tell. To do her justice, it very often did.

She'd have loved the confetti and the presentation of horseshoes in the porch and the procession to the lychgate through the gravestones. Grandma was particularly fond of those. She liked reading the inscriptions aloud in a voice like Sara Bernhardt's. She'd never have been able to resist it at a wedding.

She'd have enjoyed the reception, too, to begin with. I can picture it still myself. The flagstoned farmhouse kitchen, vast, low-ceilinged and dim, lightened by the whiteness of an enormous damask cloth that covered an equally enormous table. Gleaming glasses and cutlery, cruet after cruet — Mrs Martin must have been polishing for weeks. A three-tiered cake in the middle. Gladioli and gypsophila in cut-glass vases. There were no W.I. flower-arranging classes then.

Around this eye-catching centrepiece was the paraphernalia of everyday life. A black-leaded range, a fire in it even in August, a miscellany of china dogs, brass candlesticks, a beaded pincushion and a tin tea-caddy on the shelf above it. Old-fashioned pictures on the wall: a lady in a muslin dress poling a punt through water-lilies, another leaning pensively on a stile, both with ethereal expressions on their faces and hair piled up like haystacks. A shotgun on a rack. A corn merchant's calendar with a pocket for notes on the front of it. A framed photograph of a man in a billycock hat standing by a horse and cart.

In a glass case on a side table were four stuffed moles on a plaster molehill stuck with tufts of withered moss and yellowed grass. They'd been caught by Enna's father and one of them was cream-coloured. Very rare, he told me proudly.

Forty years out of fashion in town, Victoriana still persisted doggedly in the country—at any rate in the farmhouses and cottages. It was different with the younger gentry, whose taste for Tiffany lampshades, fumed oak and cocktail cabinets was leading to changes in some of the larger houses.

Thus it was that along one wall of the Martins' kitchen was an enormous mahogany sideboard which, Enna's mother was proudly explaining to guest after guest as they came through the doorway, had come from the previous week's sale up at the Grange. The owner had died, the house was being sold, none of his children wanted such old-fashioned furniture. The Martins had got the sideboard for three pounds on account of its size. Brass-handled, triple bow-fronted, eight feet long if it was an inch, even at the farm it was too big for any room except the kitchen.

It stood there now on the flagstones, a rag rug in front of it, a bargain by any standards. That wasn't why Mrs Martin was looking so pleased with herself, however. I realised that even at my age. It was because the sideboard had come from the Grange. A superior piece of furniture, not a throw-out from the servants' quarters, it had been used by the Family. Possessing it, by her lights, raised her own standing considerably. It was almost like being related.

Loaded with plates of chicken and ham, huge bowls of salad, jellies, trifles, bottles of sherry and yet more bowls of yellow-crusted cream, the sideboard certainly impressed its presence on the gathering, and what with that and the fact that the Rector was among the guests, Mrs Martin's social cup was overflowing.

I learned later, when I got to know the village better, that it was usual for the Rector to do this. If you got married at twelve o'clock, he expected to come to the reception. It saved his wife having to get him lunch and was a satisfactory arrangement all round. He got his lunch for nothing, and you got him on the photographs of the cake-cutting.

It was an up-mark, nevertheless, and I was suitably overawed, particularly when he sat next to me. Apparently he thought I was one of the bridesmaids in my blue satin dress. Actually I thought that was rather dim of him. Hadn't he noticed my panama? Didn't he appreciate my superior-to-any-bridesmaid status? He was important, though. It was like sitting next to God. Parsons didn't go to wedding receptions in town. He was jolly, too. He was having his glass refilled. I was beginning to like this country business. The friendly atmosphere. The Pickwickian display of food. The hills rising in the distance through the window. This was far, far better than dull old town streets. Out there lay the promise of adventure.

Adventure, in fact, was much closer at hand than that, as I discovered a short while later. By this time the Rector had left in a flurry of flapping surplice. He had another wedding at two. It seemed Bank Holiday was a favourite time for getting married in the country: the one day when, after the milking was done, the farming community had the day off en bloc and could launch you into matrimony in style.

They were hard at it at the Martins, now that the Rector had gone. Collars had been loosened. Cider jugs were going round. Faces were getting redder, voices louder. They were discussing the prospects for the village football team in the season about to start. 'Think theest have the strength to play next Saturday?' somebody bawled up the table at the bridegroom. He perspired. Enna blushed. There was a burst of raucous laughter. What did they mean, would he have the strength? I wondered. He looked strong enough to me.

'Look at old John, then!' I did and nearly dropped. There he was with his arm around Louisa. Her bridesmaid's cloche was even lower over her eyes. That, I realised, was the sherry. But sitting there giggling like a snuffed-out candle with a strange young man's arm around her? Grandma wouldn't have approved of that.

They were chaffing somebody called Dick about somebody called Dolly now. Something about meeting her in the woodshed. More hearty laughter. Mrs Martin was laughing with the rest. There was something here that wasn't quite right. This wasn't country life as Grandma had depicted it. Where the young men were clean-limbed and trustworthy, all Sir Galahads by nature (in town they were all Sir Jaspers), and the girls were innocent and pure and never used any make-up.

They might not have got round to using make-up yet, but boy, they weren't so innocent. There was one over by the stuffed moles now. In a tight pink dress surrounded by a scrum of red-faced swains. It was a wonder the glass case didn't topple over.

I was worried. Grandma definitely wouldn't have approved of that. Louisa wouldn't have either, but for the sherry. It was interesting, though. And it *was* Grandma's doing I was there. God could hardly blame me for it. On the other hand, according to Grandma, He kept a very strict eye on me. If she wasn't watching me, He was. Would He be expecting me to do something about Louisa? I decided to go and spend a penny and think about it. This solved the problem quicker than I expected. Within seconds I'd got locked in the earth-closet.

I'd never been in one before. When we'd arrived at the farm that morning Mrs Martin had shown us where the key was. About a foot long, as country keys usually were, it hung on a nail by the sink in the scullery. 'We keep it locked on account of tramps,' she said. 'It's round the corner, next to the woodshed. Mind you bolt the door when you're inside, so nobody else can walk in on you.'

Louisa visited it immediately, but I had declined, being self-conscious about such matters. Now, worried about her and having had three glasses of lemonade, I couldn't hold out any longer. I slipped out to the scullery, took down the key, and nipped quietly out and round the corner.

My goal was a stone-built outhouse with pink roses climbing over it. I got the door open easily enough. And if I'd just gone in and shot the inside bolt as Mrs Martin had said, things might have turned out very differently. Louisa might have ended up as a farmer's wife with six red-headed sons to her credit.

Instead I took the key in with me, locked the door as well as bolting it, and put the key on the seat at my side. A flat, broad seat of spotlessly scrubbed wood as spacious as a throne, it filled the back of the outhouse from wall to wall and had a pile of folded newspapers on one side of it. A comfortable seat where one could have sat and ruminated for hours, if it weren't for the decided pong, which wafted up through the hole in the middle under which was a galvanised bucket. No wonder they had roses round the door, I thought, my mind made up more quickly than I expected. I'd better go back and do something about Louisa. Obviously that was what was intended.

I put the key in the door. It turned surprisingly easily, but when I lifted the latch the door wouldn't open. I tried it again. Still no result. I was locked inside the two-foot thick stone walls as securely as if I was in the Tower of London.

I know now, after years of experience with country locks, that what I'd done was push the key right through the keyhole. There was no retaining neck to hold it in its proper place, and it was simply turning like a clock-hand on the outside.

I didn't know then that it needed manipulating with the skill of a safe-breaker until one was used to it, when it automatically became second nature. I just stood there, as near to the door as I could get so I could catch the scent of the roses, which was a good deal better than the whiff behind me. I didn't shout. The girls of Morcove wouldn't have done that, particularly in such an embarrassing situation. Something was bound to happen, I told myself, and eventually something did. Louisa surfaced from under her cloche hat and discovered that I was missing.

I can hear her now, rushing frantically into the yard and calling me. The other guests coming out after her. Mrs Martin saying there, there, I must be somewhere around. Louisa sobbing that I must have been taken by the gypsies. (Another of my grandmother's nightmares, that. She was constantly expecting me to be carried off by gypsies.)

Why didn't I shout when I heard Louisa calling? Again because I was so self-conscious. I stood there mute while the searchers milled around. Somebody tried the door and, finding it locked, obviously assumed it had a bona fide occupant. 'Sorry', said a man's voice, his footsteps passing on to inspect the woodshed and then going back along the path.

It was Mrs Martin who eventually spotted the empty key-hook and came to the door of the earth-closet and called me. She was a lady and she spoke to me quietly. It was all right to answer her. I explained what had happened. Unfortunately even then I couldn't be rescued easily by pushing the key right through the keyhole and Mrs Martin using it from the other side. The key-handle was too big to go through. Neither would the key go over the top of the door or under it. Only recently, it seemed, Mrs Martin had complained of the draught when the wind blew and Mr Martin had nailed up the gaps with strips of wood.

They had to take the door off its hinges, and Louisa's John was one of my rescuers, working away with a screw-driver with a will. He thought it tremendously funny and roared his head off when I sidled out, but I didn't and neither did Louisa, who stood there looking as if she wished the earth would swallow her up since life had nothing worse to offer.

Actually I recovered my equilibrium quite quickly. People made a fuss of me. I had some more lemonade. Enna's father gave me a ride on one of his plough-horses and showed me a litter of piglets and a ferret in a cage. I was so fascinated it was quite a while before I realised that Louisa was with us as well but there was absolutely no sign of John.

I asked where he was. She didn't know, she said. After what I'd done she couldn't look him in the face. She had to watch me anyway, or the next thing I'd fall down the well and goodness knows what Grandma'd say if she went home without me.

Quite a lot, I imagined. Anyway, we went back into the farmhouse where by this time everybody was having tea. John kept looking across at Louisa, but she wouldn't look at him. Eventually he gave it up and joined the group round the girl in pink. Then suddenly it was early evening and time for the bridal pair to leave.

Farming people didn't have honeymoons in those days. Tom and Enna were simply going to walk over to the cottage they'd got ready a mile away. Tom would be back up at his father's farm, milking by hand at 5.30 the next morning; Enna would be washing-up and doing the grate. It was romantic, all the same, their walking off along the lane in the evening sunlight, Enna in a new blue dress, carrying her bridal bouquet, Tom with confetti still on his coat. They turned at the bend to wave at the guests gathered at the gate, like Norma Shearer and Leslie Howard in *Smiling Through.*

'Be up to see thee soon,' called one young man, a member of the football team from the size of him. 'Mind theest leave thee window open.' 'Ah, we got the buckets ready,' shouted another.

Enna giggled coyly in the distance. 'Buckets?' I remember pondering. Surely they weren't going to take over yet more cider and continue the party. Tom and Enna would be wanting to have their supper.

What they did have in mind — though it was a long time before I was considered old enough to know about it — was the age-old custom of bride-bedding, where on the wedding night friends gathered under the couple's bedroom window, banging buckets and shouting encouragement. Following the tradition of royal bride-bedding, which was conducted in public down to the Prince Regent's day, it was still kept up, if somewhat less refinedly, in country districts in the twenties.

Now it was time for us to go home, too. Enna's father drove us to the station this time, the pony's hooves clip-clopping along the white-dusted lane, Louisa still very silent. The shadows were lengthening. The poppies were closed. There was a feeling of summer accomplished in the air. Swallows were diving after midges in the lane in front of us, and over the hill, behind the church, the harvest moon — pale as yet because the sun had still not set — was waiting to take over the sky.

'Gosh, it's been super,' I sighed when we were rattling back to town on the train. 'I'd like to live in the country when I grow up.'

She wouldn't said Louisa. She thought it was horrid. She wasn't ever going to go there again.

Chapter Two

Actually we were back the following Easter. In the interim Louisa had started going for cycle rides with the new curate at our local church, whose name was Harold, and she had got over looking like Ophelia when she thought of John. And as Grandma was now keeping a weather eye on Harold, who was hanging around far too much for her liking, any invitation which removed Louisa from the target area for a while was obviously to be encouraged.

Thus, when Louisa said she couldn't possibly go away for Easter, what with all the services and she always helped with the Easter flowers — and she couldn't leave Grandma for three whole days, she added hastily, in case our progenitor got the wrong impression — Grandma, who usually went all tottery in such a situation, announcing that she wouldn't be with us much longer now, Louisa must go if she wished, of course, she only hoped her loved ones were all present when she returned; Grandma, in a hearty, live-to-be-a-hundred voice, now said rubbish, it would do her good. It would do me good, too. Hadn't she noticed how pale I looked? Really, she couldn't think how Louisa could be so selfish.

Louisa, who was about the most unselfish person one could hope to meet, acquiesced at once. Enna's invitation had included me, of course. She'd remembered her previous encounter with Grandma. And so it was that Easter Saturday saw us country-bound again, this time on a bus which stopped conveniently at the end of the steep, narrow lane up which was Tom and Enna's cottage.

It was on this trip I discovered that bus rides made me sick. At least they did if I read *True Westerns* all the way, as was my habit when we went by train. When we went on holiday with my grandmother, we always travelled by train — the station was near us, she'd been used to trains since her childhood, she considered them a whole lot safer. It was the fact of the bus-stop being at the end of Enna's lane that led her to decide that this time we should go by road. We could run up it if anyone tried to accost us when we got off, she said, and she would have a word with the conductor. She did — about how we were travelling on our own and me being an orphan and would he see that we got off at the right stop. You'd think we were going to Istanbul on the Orient Express instead of fifteen miles down the Bridgwater Road.

He saw to it that we got off all right. By the time we reached the village I must have been looking pretty green. He'd been watching me anxiously for quite a while — he

could hardly wait to pull the stopping bell. 'She'll be all right now,' he said to Louisa, manoeuvring me speedily down the bus step and on to the grass. 'Just walk her about and give her some air.' He was up the step again and the bus had gone. I had a vague remembrance of seeing him peering through the back window, no doubt thinking that had been a close one.

Poor Louisa. I remember her, too, struggling to hold me up, saying why was it Grandma and I always seemed to conspire to do our worst. I thought it a bit unfeeling at the time, but, looking back, it was pretty hard on her, marooned out in the wilds, holding me up like a sagging flagpole when she could have been putting primroses round the font with Harold.

Help was at hand, however. Enna was hurrying down to meet us. Between them they got me up the lane to the cottage. A cup of tea and an Easter cake and I was as right as rain, bursting with enthusiasm for everything.

Actually they overdid the Easter cakes a bit. We had them everywhere we went that weekend. For tea at Enna's. For supper at the Martins' farm that night after large helpings of cauliflower cheese. On the way home we called on Enna's Aunt Florrie. She gave us Easter cakes and dandelion wine. Both Louisa and I lay awake clutching our stomachs that night, having eaten what felt like dozens of them.

There seemed to be some sort of rivalry about them — we were pressed to try everybody's and say what we thought. Enna's were burnt and tasted odd — they were the first ones she'd ever made. Mrs Martin's were underdone. The fire in the range had gone out while her back was turned — probably while she was rolling out more of them. Aunt Florrie's were so tough you could have tiled the floor with them. The ones we had at Enna's Uncle Walter's after church next morning were a peculiar greyish-pink. His wife, Aunt Allie, said she'd run out of yellow colouring after her first three batches and had used cochineal instead.

It made no difference. These people were all so friendly, so hospitable, we *had* to eat their cakes and say they were nice. Why were they so frenetic about it, though? Was it simply competition? Or did it go deeper than that?

I have a theory. This was King Alfred's country: ancient Wessex. It was in these parts that he fought the Danes. Remember the story of how, after he was defeated by Guthrum, he took refuge in a peasant's hut? How the old woman, not knowing who he was, told him to watch the cakes while she was out—and Alfred, cogitating how to beat Guthrum the next time they met (which he did), forgot them and they burned to a cinder?

It could be that Somerset housewives have always been compulsive cake-makers. I mean, fancy making them right after a battle. Vikings rushing round yelling about Thor and Odin; battle-axes clanking; horses whinnying, raven banners flying; defeated Saxons fleeing across the peat-rhines—and in the middle of it all, in a hut, cool as a cucumber, an old lady nonchalantly making cakes. I remember an artist's impression of the scene in my junior history reader. Flat cakes baked on a griddle, looking just like Easter cakes. I reckon they've had a mania for making them ever since. I only hope Alfred hadn't to eat as many of them as we did.

I didn't know about this being Dane country then, of course, though Enna was a mine of information on local legend. She took us up to the grass-covered ramparts on Dolbury Hill, which she said the Romans had built in a night. They'd have had a job to put that lot up in a night! Some of the walls were twenty feet high. Later we learned that it was actually an Iron Age fort, occupied by the Romans when they came and later by the Danes—as important, according to one historian, as Troy had been in ancient Greece, guarding the ancient trade-route to the Mendip lead mines.

No matter. Enna's story was fascinating enough and

there was some truth in it, though it was garbled. I walked the ramparts feeling I'd been transported back through time, imagining the chariots, the standards, the centurions ... Tom had found an arrow-head in a rabbit burrow up here as a boy, Enna told us. I searched dozens of burrow entrances but I couldn't find one. What I did find — representative of a superstition far older than the Romans, though Enna didn't know it and neither did I at the time — was what looked like a stone with a hole through it. Enna said if you found one on Dolbury it was supposed to be lucky. Actually mine wasn't really a stone. It was a piece of metallic ore with a hole through it. Enna said she expected it would count.

Another day we walked to a neighbouring village along a lane past a field full of jonquils. Enna said they'd been brought home from the Crusades by a local knight. He'd come back to find his wife had died of a broken heart in his absence. He'd planted the jonquils, then he died too. The jonquils had flowered there ever since. A poignant tale, though an inscription on a monument in the church sets the incident, minus the jonquils, in the Civil War. Crusade or Civil War, it is all the same by country reckoning. All past, all merging, nothing forgotten. Jonquils do grow wild in the Holy Land. They could have been part of another story.

Even so, they had been planted by human hands. It was the valley of daffodils that captured me. We walked up through it on Sunday morning on our way to church, over the stile at the top of Enna's lane. The ground was oddly pock-marked, like the surface of the moon. Enna said that years ago they'd mined for calamine there and these were the surface diggings.

Long overgrown by the Mendip turf, nothing could have been further now from the concept of mining. Rabbits dashed across our path on urgent errands; violets sunned themselves on damp-mossed banks; celandines shone their enamelled yellow; larks, their songs lifting with them, rose towards the blue spring sky. There was a feeling of seclusion, of being far from the rest of the world, even while ahead of us the Easter bells were ringing.

And all around us there were daffodils. It was the loveliest sight I had ever seen. Miniature daffodils, about six inches high, rising from clumps of perfect, miniature leaves. Everywhere. Poised like conquerors on top of the abandoned diggings, clustered thickly in the shelter of the hollows. Daffodils in flower, with toy-sized trumpets: daffodils in bud by the thousand. They were wild, said Enna, who was used to the sight. People said they'd always been here.

It was a triumph of quiet persistence. They must have been dug in consistently during the hundred years or so when this was mining land. And still, when the miners went, the daffodils came back, working their patient way up from the depths. The daffodils, the cascades of catkins, the leaping, black-faced lambs — the countryside was young, and I was young, and I revelled in it all.

The cottage was old, though, and I revelled in that too — even more than the Martins' farm. It was built into the hillside, and Louisa's and my bedroom window opened on to a bank of ferns and moss at the back. It meant that the cottage was damp — it had to be papered every year — but it certainly made one feel part of the country. The moment you woke up you cast an eye over the patchwork quilt and there it was, right outside your window.

The cottage had a gorgeous smell of oil-lamps and polish and baking. It was so small it had no parlour: just a kitchen-cum-living room with a tiny scullery attached and two small bedrooms above. Thus, when Emma cooked the breakfast in the morning — bacon from Tom's father's or the Martins' pigs, eggs from the dozen Rhode Island Reds clucking contentedly in a run halfway down the garden — the mouth-watering smell and the sound of the sizzling rose straight up through the warped oak floorboards to where Louisa and I were washing. In an old-fashioned washbasin filled from an old-fashioned pitcher which, in turn, was filled from an old-fashioned pump in the yard.

Enna didn't think much of the cottage. She and Tom were waiting for one of the bigger farm cottages to become vacant — or, better still, if they could persuade Tom's father to build one, she would like to have a bungalow. With a bathroom, she said. A proper kitchen with a proper stove. Electricity, not smelly old oil lamps. And two proper lavatories, one in and one outside, not a tumbledown earth-closet down the lane.

I agreed about the earth-closet. Here it was even more an outpost of Empire than at the Martins, the garden being a long, narrow strip beneath the hill. To get to the privy you went out of the front gate and about twenty yards down the lane, carrying the usual enormous key. Not only was it a long way if you happened to be in a hurry, but everybody you met knew where you were going.

'Mustn't keep 'ee me dear,' said one old man one morning, stopping to talk to me, noticing the key and plodding tactfully on his way. Tactful he may have been, but I was mortified. I didn't like earth-closets one bit. For the rest, though, the countryside, the peaceful cottage with its thick stone walls and oil-lamps, the feeling of history, of continuity, of being self-sufficient... One day, I confided euphorically to Louisa, *I* was going to live in a cottage like this. I'd probably go in for making Easter cakes too, said Louisa. Knowing me she wouldn't mind betting on it.

Louisa still didn't like the country very much. Over the weekend she'd had her first encounter with cows. Enna had taken us to Tom's father's farm for tea one afternoon by a footpath that went through the fields, and the herd — sixty or so large Devon Reds — happened to be grazing in one of them.

We'd never met cows at close quarters before. Seen from the train window en route to the seaside for our annual summer holiday they were one thing: placid, picturesque, part of the rural landscape. Met up with blocking the footpath, life-sized and with horns like hayforks (most cows had horns in those days), one of them had only to look at Louisa and moo companionably and she was up the nearest cider apple tree in a flash. I didn't know she could climb like that. She certainly couldn't get down again. We had to fetch Tom and his father and a ladder. When she was down, the four of us had to escort her across the field in a protective scrum and she had to be given brandy — plus an Easter cake — at the end of it. 'They were *bulls*... they had *horns*... she kept saying hysterically.

It was no good Enna explaining to her how one really distinguished a bull. Louisa said she didn't intend going close enough in future to be able to look. It struck me that Grandma would consider this conversation indelicate, would probably never allow us near the country again if she heard about it. So I didn't mention the incident when we got back to town. Louisa didn't, because she couldn't possibly have repeated what Enna had told her. Grandma went on imagining we spent our time breathing the country air and picking buttercups — and at Whitsun we were back again.

And in August, for Tom and Enna's anniversary, and again for Harvest Festival. Only for the day on these latter occasions, going out and back by bus. Louisa could stand that, and Enna liked having us, and Grandma considered even a day away from Harold well worthwhile from a long-term viewpoint.

I asked Louisa only recently how she came to be friends with Enna in the first place. She wasn't a relation and we had no other connections with the country. How was it, too, that Grandma let us go out there so trustingly when she'd never met the elder Martins herself? Usually she watched over us as if we were a couple of dopey daisies liable to be snatched by white slavers at any moment.

On such small things does the course of life depend. Louisa said that during the First World War her older brother Franklyn's fiancée Grace had insisted on working on munitions. She was hopeless at it, said Louisa. She'd nearly blown the factory up. However, that had nothing to do with it. Grace was an orphan and lodged with a widow, a Mrs Wilson, Franklyn being in the army at the time, and Mrs Wilson in turn had an admirer — Enna's Uncle Walter. She didn't marry him in the end, and Louisa didn't know how he'd come into the picture in the first place — only that he was there quite often when she called for Grace, who was ten years older than she was and was allowed to take her out to tea. (Here, quietly safeguarding Franklyn's interests, we again see the hand of Grandma.)

Louisa said Enna's Uncle Walter usually had his feet in a bowl when she saw him. It seems he always walked the fifteen miles to town. Presumably to show the extent of his devotion to Mrs Wilson, since he could easily have come in by carrier's cart. It didn't get him very far. She eventually married a train driver who demonstrated *his* devotion by taking her to the cinema twice a week and to Weston-super-Mare on his free pass on his day off, and Uncle Walter married Allie — who lived next door to him in the village — and saved himself an awful lot of walking.

That is by the way, however. While he was still courting

Mrs Wilson, she had Enna in to stay with her once or twice, and Louisa met Enna through going round to call for Grace, and the two teenagers became friends. They wrote to each other — a procedure beamed on by Grandma with her concept of the wholesome, innocent influence of country life. Country people didn't travel very much in those days, and after the break-up between Mrs Wilson and Uncle Walter, Enna and Louisa didn't actually meet again for several years. Then Enna came to stay for a week. She was eighteen at the time, and wore her hair in a bun, no make-up and calf-length skirts. Definitely the type of which Grandma approved. She said so to Louisa. Enna was a properly brought-up old-fashioned girl, she said. *She'd* never get into trouble.

On the strength of this, when Enna got married Louisa was allowed to be her bridesmaid without question. Grandma had still not met Enna's parents — it was to be years before she did — but they were country people. They *must* be nice. (Actually they were.) And so it was that Louisa and I, whom she guarded like a mother eagle when we were in town, were permitted — *pushed*, when Harold appeared on the scene — to visit Enna any time she asked us, without question. Grandma thought country life was innocent and soulful: all church-going and churning butter and dancing round the maypole on May Day morning. Which only shows what Grandma knew, as we very soon discovered.

Chapter Three

According to my grandmother, the thing most likely to bring about a young girl's downfall — other than the white slavers who lay in wait round every corner in town — was when she started going to dances and staying out after eleven o'clock.

It led irrevocably to fast living. To the use of lipstick, smoking and riding pillion on the back of motor-bikes. A brief spell of this and you then either had to get married (in which case your husband would never respect you), or you ended a broken butterfly in the gutter, most probably selling matches.

Why eleven o'clock was the deadline was a mystery I never solved. Dances, after all, took place mostly in the winter. It was dark before the dance even started. If anyone had a fancy to tread the primrose park in the local park, they didn't need to wait until eleven.

It made no difference. A social that finished at half-past ten was perfectly all right. Louisa went to that with Grandma's blessing. A dance that ended at midnight with girls in men's arms — even if it was in the Scout Hut in aid of roof repairs — was the first step to perdition.

In vain Louisa protested, on the few occasions that she went, that she hadn't been in *men's* arms, she'd only danced with Harold. That was what Grandma was afraid of. Harold was getting too close in more ways than one. Dances were definitely to be discouraged.

She was so adamant about this — Louisa was in the doghouse for days if she so much as suggested the possibility of going to a Scout hop — that when I mentioned that Enna and Tom had gone to a dance while we were with them (in the W.I. Hall in aid of the football club) but, I hastily assured her, Louisa and I had spent the evening at Enna's mother's playing dominoes, I nearly fell through the floor when Grandma asked why on earth we hadn't gone too?

It seems that another of her convictions was that in the country they still did country dancing: all skipping, bouncing, clapping hands and never actually getting to grips. You could hardly sneak off with your partner, either, when it needed eight of you to make a set.

I said that Enna said it was a *proper* dance. Of course it was, said Grandma. Enna was a country girl — that was what she *would* call proper dancing. Really, education nowadays — they didn't teach much commonsense.

So the next time we went to stay with Enna we took our party dresses. I had my blue satin that I'd worn for the wedding, and Louisa took her pale pink taffeta printed with cabbage roses. But if Grandma fondly pictured us doing the Shepherd's Hey on Saturday night, then Grandma was sadly mistaken.

The setting was countrified all right. They'd scrubbed the floor of the hall for a start instead of polishing it, so that while it looked as fresh as a dairy and was a credit to the ladies who did it, it was impossible to glide on it at all. This, and the fact that most of the men were self-conscious anyway, resulted in the dancing having a most peculiar motion. People were going round lifting their knees as if they were trampling straw, bringing them down again like a herd of elephants.

It was countrified, too, in that I was permitted to attend, which certainly wouldn't have happened in town. I danced most of the dances with Enna — to give Louisa a chance to meet some of the nice young men, Enna explained confidingly. Enna was tall, and I had to take long strides to try

to match her steps. It couldn't have been much fun for her, but I was beside myself with importance, attending my very first dance.

Louisa was beside herself for a different reason. After a while the nice young men started nipping off for refreshment. Not, as in the Scout Hut at home, for lemonade from a trestle table in the corner by the piano. This lot kept going down the lane to the Dog and Duck, where they quaffed their mugs of cider, no doubt boasted to one another of their conquests, and returned refreshed and emboldened to the fray. Even the most sheepish of them gradually became more lion-like. A few such visits and some of them were positively wolves. They began competing to partner Louisa, the girl from the city, and the dancing was anything but decorous. They were using Excuse Me dance tactics even in an ordinary foxtrot: tapping one another on the shoulder, whisking her off as if they'd won her in a hoop-la, grinning triumphantly at their rivals until, in turn, somebody grabbed her from behind. Poor Louisa was going round like a Whirling Dervish. It was certainly different from dancing with Harold.

I began to get anxious. I felt responsible for Louisa. I manoeuvred Enna as close to her as I could. At this point she was being propelled round by an individual even more alarming-looking than the rest, with a round red face like an apoplectic beetroot, a grin like an advertisement for tombstones, and eyes like bottle stoppers. I nearly dropped when, as we passed, I heard him ask in a treacly voice, 'Be you Mary Pickford?' Louisa said she wasn't, but he took no notice. 'I be Douglas Fairbanks,' he informed her, leering at her from ear to ear.

A maniac, I thought. Honestly, the things Louisa could get into. Enna assured me it was quite all right. He was just a bit simple: his world revolved around film stars and he never missed the travelling cinema on Friday nights. His name was Ernie Douglas, so the village had taken to calling

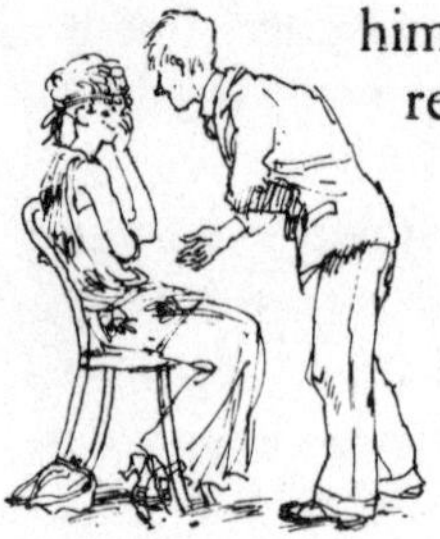

him Douglas Fairbanks. He knew he wasn't really, of course.

Did he, though? He was looking pretty passionately at Louisa. I imagined him slinging her over his shoulder at any moment. This was where I took a hand. 'I have to dance with my aunt,' I announced, pushing between them, grabbing her and starting off in a waltz like a juvenile Groucho Marx. Normally Louisa didn't like me telling people she was my aunt. It made her sound so old, she said. She was happy to be called aunt for the rest of that evening, though. I helped keep off the wolves.

Some of them were wolves, too—or the inevitable manifestation of youth, if you looked at it another way. Grandma would have dropped if she could have seen, as the evening wore on, the number of girls who giggled out through the side door escorted by smirking swains and returned later giggling more than ever.

We didn't tell her about this when we got back to town—or about the foxtrotting and Douglas Fairbanks. I wanted to go on visiting the country and, while Louisa wasn't particularly worried about that, she certainly didn't want my grandmother turning up at our own church events, keeping a gimlet eye on Harold in case he suddenly decided he was Ramon Novarro.

Feeling on the other hand—having been rigidly instructed by her in moral principles—that it would be wrong to continue going to something we knew she wouldn't have approved of (wild horses wouldn't have dragged Louisa to another village dance in any case, not with Ernie Douglas in prospect), we merely said we hadn't liked the dance very much: it was far too fast

for us. Of course it was fast, said Grandma, more correctly than she realised. That was what country dancing was all *about*.

No doubt it always had been. Dancing merry dances at the Midsummer Fair, wandering off afterwards into the hayfields, the moon shining down on a romantic fairyland perfumed by honeysuckle and the fragrance of the sun-warmed beanfields. Many a girl was married as a result by Christmas and a mother when the spring came round. Read Chaucer, Shakespeare, Fielding's *Tom Jones*—human nature was ever thus, and in the country, whatever the parson said in church, they didn't consider it too much of a fall from grace, so long as the couple got married in good time and brought their children up to be God-fearing. Some of the most sober families in the village, according to Enna who knew all their histories, were the outcome of a stroll long ago through the mowing grass on a summer evening, with a cuckoo calling encouragingly from a may tree.

It was going on still. Dick and Dolly, for instance, of whom I'd heard first at Enna's wedding: he was a cowman who lived-in at the Martins' farm, she was a housemaid at the Manor. They attended church on Sunday evenings—he was in the choir—and afterwards went for a stroll around the local lanes. We met them once: Dick in a blue serge suit with Sunday-pomaded hair, looking uncomfortable in a collar and tie and shiny boots; Dolly a little mouse of a thing, hardly up to his shoulder, wearing a straight grey coat, lace-up shoes and an old-maidish straw hat like a plate.

She *was* an old maid. Forty, Enna told us: and Dick was twenty-seven. No wonder people chaffed them, I thought. Forty and twenty-seven! It was ludicrous. She looked so prim. Nobody could possibly feel romantic about *her*. It was mean of people, I decided, making jokes like that about the woodshed, almost as if they were trying to encourage them.

Probably they were. Dolly was a worthy little soul who

longed for marriage and children but had seen the years slip past without her getting them. Dick was stolid, slow in the uptake, looking older than his years. She had smiled at him, he had responded, two lonely people had come together; and if rainy weather led to their sheltering in the Martins' woodshed on Sunday nights and eventually to affection, which it obviously did, since in due course, sure enough, Dick and Dolly had to get married . . . It was time Dick had somebody to take care of him, said the village; a young girl wouldn't have looked at him — and Dolly, after all her waiting, was getting the home and family she'd always wanted. Quite a satisfactory arrangement, all things considered — with a little encouragement from the village.

My grandmother would probably have thought so too. She had considerable understanding. It was just that she wanted to make sure that her own girls — Louisa and myself — would never find themselves in such a position. She succeeded so well that Louisa, in fact, never did get married. Me? In due course I was to marry Charles, of whom Grandma approved so much that, as she was always telling me, if she'd been forty years younger she'd have married him herself and I wouldn't have got a look in.

This is jumping ahead, however. Let us return to the end of the twenties when I was eleven, Louisa was twenty-four and Enna, newly-married to her Tom, had similar designs for her friend. To this end she took us over one day to the Fosters' farm. It was John Foster who had been best man at her wedding. He'd obviously been smitten with Louisa and she with him until I mucked things up by getting locked in the earth-closet.

She didn't say we were going to visit John. She just said it was Mrs Foster's butter-making day and she thought we might like to watch. Ostensibly it was just chance that, as we passed the open door of one of the farm buildings, John should be inside about to start making cheese. We hadn't seen him since the day of Enna's wedding; he hadn't been at the football club dance and after all this time even Louisa could scarcely blush about his unscrewing the earth-closet door more than a year before.

So we went in and stood watching while, handsome as a film star playing the part of a surgeon in his white coat and round white hat, he added rennet to a big wooden tub of milk, stirred it till it coagulated, and left it until the curd was formed. Then he cut it into sections, drew off the whey, and cut the curd into blocks again for ripening. Ripening could take hours, John explained at this point, after which it would have to be minced, have salt added to it and be put into a press. We couldn't wait that long, of course, so with a blush or two from Louisa, an ardent look from John, plus a scooped-out taste of Cheddar from a finished cheese, we passed on to the dairy where Mrs Foster was waiting for us, ready to embark upon the butter.

I'm afraid that did it. As Mrs Foster warmed to her subject — twelve gallons of milk produced two-and-a-half gallons of cream, she told us, which in turn produced twenty pounds of butter (she accompanied this pronouncement by pouring the cream into a butter churn, which looked like a barrel with a handle on it, and started turning it like a mangle) — Louisa began to look as apprehensive as a fly seeing a spider approaching purposefully down a web.

It was the realisation of what a farmer's wife *did*. She made butter twice a week like this, Mrs Foster panted breathlessly, meantime changing over churning hands. Took it to market ... This was her pin-money ... This and looking after the hens ... On she churned. Would Louisa like a turn? she asked. Louisa reluctantly had a go. A couple of cranks and she was practically revolving with the handle. Grandma always said she hadn't much stamina.

'You'd soon get used to it,' Mrs Foster said encouragingly, probably only by way of conversation. I don't suppose she knew which way the wind was blowing — or might have blown but for Louisa seeing the butter-making.

But Louisa obviously took it personally. She saw the trapdoor closing. Herself in this very dairy churning butter twice a week. Herself endlessly feeding ducks and chickens. Herself clattering about in clogs, like Mrs Foster, to keep her feet off the constantly-washed-down floor.

'I wouldn't,' she said. 'I don't like cows.' With which her romance with John finally ended.

We went on visiting the country, though. Grandma still wasn't taking chances with Harold, Louisa and Enna were very great friends, and I loved every minute of it and was always announcing that when I grew up I was going to live in this very village.

One day we came down from Dolbury, which was one of my favourite places, by way of a path that led down to a wooded valley and a stream, then across it and up a hill on the other side. There was a whitewashed cottage by the stream crossing, set back a little from the lane. I didn't take much notice of it — people were living in that one. It was two other cottages that caught my eye. We looked down at them as we climbed the track up the hill. They were set sideways-on beneath us and were obviously empty. The people who'd lived there had moved out to council houses, said Enna. Nobody wanted to live down here.

There was no electricity. The water came from the stream. The valley itself was too remote. The cottages had been built by miners a century and a half before, in the days of the calamine diggings. The calamine had petered out, the miners had gone. Some folk had stayed on in the cottages, but as they died the Squire, on whose land the cottages had been built, had stripped off the roofs so that the cottages couldn't be passed on to their descendants. Most of whom didn't want them anyway, now that they could have council houses in the village proper with bathrooms and all mod cons.

The young squire took a different view from his father. He was willing to rent out such cottages as remained intact to anyone who wanted them. 'For five shillings a week,' said Enna as we looked down at them. 'But who'd want to live down there?'

I would. I can see myself looking down at them now, picturing us coming out there every weekend. Five shillings a week was a lot more than my sixpence pocket money, but I was willing to contribute that if it would help. I tried to convert Louisa to the idea on the way back to town on the bus, but Louisa wasn't having any. I told my grandmother — she was always saying she'd like to live in the country herself — but she said she didn't believe in renting property.

She came out with us to Enna's once, but we didn't go near the valley. He visited the Martins' farm and then we went for a walk round the village, where she saw a field for sale. She decided she *would* like that: land, she said, was a good investment. We could keep a cow there and have our own milk. 'Where would we live?' I asked excitedly, thinking my dream was coming true at last. 'In town of course,' she said. We still had my schooling to think of. Her brother William could come out on the bus every day and milk it and bring the milk back to town.

We were still trying to persuade her out of that one — she talked for years afterwards of how, if she'd bought that field, we'd have had a herd of cows by now — when we came to the village antique shop where, immediately forgetting all else, my grandmother spotted a china bedpan.

I have told this story before* about my grandmother considering herself the family Florence Nightingale and believing in being prepared for emergencies, to which end she'd acquired over the years an assortment of nursing requisites ranging from two night commodes to a back-rest and a feeding cup. The one thing missing from her disaster kit, as she realised the moment she saw it, was a bedpan like the one in the window. For use, she explained, gazing

* In *Life With Grandma*: Elek Books, 1964.

raptly at it, if anybody was too ill to get to the commode. She bought it. The shop-owner wrapped it as best he could in newspaper, apologising for the fact that the ends didn't meet. Not only had we to accompany her through the village carrying a bedpan sticking out of newspaper, but there was still worse to come.

Enna gave us some of her cowslip wine that evening, while we waited for it to be time to catch the bus. Grandma and Louisa had a tumblerful each, pronouncing it to be a beautiful colour and very warming. I was given half a sherry glass. Just like grown-ups, I thought. It only tasted like soppy old water. Why couldn't I have a proper glass?

It was just as well I didn't. We set out alone on the walk down to the bus-stop. By this time it was raining slightly, and there seemed no point in Enna getting wet as well. 'No,' said Grandma, refusing the offer of an umbrella. 'It isn't heavy enough for that.'

It was by the time we got halfway down the lane. It was coming down in buckets. The newspaper round the bed-pan, which Grandma was carrying, was soggy and hanging in strips. Louisa, at her side, carried a box of eggs. I had a bunch of pinks. The rain beat relentlessly down on us, soaking our flimsy dresses.

It was at this stage that Louisa turned to say something and noticed that my grandmother's straw hat had gone funny in the rain. The crown had risen to a point, and the brim had shrunk and was wavy and all turned down. Normally Louisa would have been horrified, but now she started pointing and giggling helplessly. It was Enna's cowslip wine, of course: it certainly had been warming.

Grandma took one look at Louisa and started laughing too. Louisa's hat — a white felt shovel-brimmed affair with a bow at the back — had shrunk in the rain as well. What was more Louisa, under the influence of the cowslip wine, had put it on back to front. She now appeared to be wearing a dustman's hat, several sizes too small, in wet white felt with a soggy white bow dangling limply over her forehead.

My panama had shrunk, too, but they didn't notice me. Hysterically they made it to the bus-stop. Hysterically, when the bus came, they laughed themselves aboard, my grandmother, to the interest of the other passengers, carrying a now completely unwrapped bedpan. Sitting behind them holding my sodden bunch of pinks, I tried hard to look as if I wasn't with them though conscious of the fact that I only too obviously was — conscious, too, from my reflection in the bus window, that my panama now looked as if I was a native of Tibet! This wouldn't have happened at Morcove, I thought. I wished I went to boarding school.

Chapter Four

The years slipped past. I passed my matric, left grammar school, and took a course at a commercial college. I dreamed of going to university, but my grandmother could never have afforded it.

Harold had departed long ago to be a missionary in Hong Kong. Louisa was learning Esperanto. She liked hobbies that improved her mind and my grandmother encouraged her in them. Presumably to keep her occupied and away from man's base designs, though it didn't always work out like that.

Anyway, Louisa was peacefully studying Esperanto and I was eighteen and looking for a job. I still dreamed of adventure. Of living in the country, where people were individuals. Of visiting foreign places. Of living on a ranch, like the heroines in the *True Westerns* I still read, riding the range on a cow-pony, meeting up with coyotes and bears. I was to do all of these in due course, though there seemed little prospect of it then. In the late thirties, girls like me went into offices, where the nearest thing to a bear was the boss.

After a couple of jobs I hated for their dullness, I joined a big industrial company and stayed with them for years. As a typist. As a secretary. Later, when they discovered I could write, in their public relations department. I was still with them when I wrote my first book, *Cats In the Belfry*, but again this is jumping ahead. It was in that firm, just as war broke out, that I met Charles, whom I was to marry. The company's Head Office was enormous. Charles was in the Accountants' Department, lofty and secluded, and for two years we never encountered each other. But we passed one day on the staircase — not an ordinary staircase, I must point out, but a wide, imposing affair of panelled oak with richly carved newel posts, as befitted a prosperous firm with old traditions. It could equally well have been a staircase in a big country house: there was nothing unromantic about the setting.

We went to the cinema that night to see *The Last Of The Mohicans*, and afterwards we had coffee and Charles drove me home. In a sports car that had what must have been the noisiest exhaust in England and was Charles's pride and joy. After that, until he went off to war some six months later, it roared down the street several times a week. A signal to me that he was arriving, nearly always late: Charles was as unpunctual then as ever since. A signal to my grandmother, lying awake around midnight, that the dear boy, as she called him, was bringing me safely home. (Charles could get away with anything as far as she was concerned: there was no 10.30 curfew for me.) A signal to the neighbours, hearing him zoom round the block after leaving me — it was a rectangular block with large gardens behind it, and you could hear him brrm-brrming all the way round — that the young chap in the plus fours and white leather driving helmet, who looked a bit like Maurice Chevalier, had finished disturbing the peace for the night and now they could get some *sleep*.

Had I forgotten my dreams so soon? Not by any means.

Charles, too, loved the country and wanted to live in it one day. He, too, wanted to travel. He had been born in Canada, as a child he had crossed the prairies, and he wanted to see it all again. Over a meal, or coffee after the cinema, the two of us now dreamed of such things together.

Meanwhile at weekends we drove into the country as far as petrol rationing permitted and Charles took me on his favourite walks. At the end of every walk was a place where we would have tea and where Charles appeared to be very well known. One was a farmhouse; another was a village tea-room run by two spinster sisters; another was a cottage on a hillside overlooking a lake. At each of them elderly ladies fluttered out, greeted Charles with coy delight, ushered us inside and said they expected he'd like the usual. This, when it appeared, consisted of two boiled eggs apiece, brown bread and butter, home-made fruit cake, and pineapple chunks, for which it seemed Charles had a passion after a walk.

Such was the effect of his happy beam upon dear old ladies, that long after eggs were rationed in town, long after pineapple chunks were but a memory to most people, we only had to turn up at one of his tea-places and they appeared as if by magic. I think the sisters at the tea-room must have had a case of chunks specially reserved for him. They kept them going the longest. They produced their very last tin, by odd coincidence, on our last walk before Charles joined the Navy. There wouldn't be any more until the war was over, they said regretfully, hovering to watch him enjoy them. We wouldn't be back again till then ourselves, Charles told them. But not to worry, it wouldn't be long.

So Charles went to war, laying his sports car up for the duration — undoubtedly to the relief of the neighbours. They were losing enough sleep by that time getting up for the first of the air-raids, without being blasted from their beds by his exhaust. When he came home on weekend passes, we went to the country by bus — though not so far afield as we used to go. When he couldn't get home, I spent my weekends making cakes for him, posting them off on Monday morning. I wasn't exactly the best of cooks, as readers of *Life With Grandma* may remember. But mixed with the hand of love and watched over by my grandmother lest they burned, how could I go wrong with a batch of rock cakes? They looked all right anyway, and Charles wrote saying they were super and, gosh, wasn't I clever to be able to make them.

Emboldened, after several such consignments, I made a cherry cake. The cherries sank to the bottom to a man. It burned a bit too, Grandma having gone out into the garden and forgotten it, but I hoped for the best and sent it off. Charles wrote thanking me. It hardly seemed possible, he said, that one day I'd be cooking just like that for him out on the prairie.

He maintains to this day that he meant it that way and wasn't being funny. At that besotted stage, he says, he thought it wonderful of me even to be able to light an oven. Not for anything would he have told me that the cakes were like fossilised granite.

The truth came to light on account of my sending the cakes to him packed in biscuit tins. I got the tins from the grocer, but they were becoming scarcer and anyway they cost me half-a-crown each. Couldn't he bring them back when he came on leave so I could use them again? I kept asking. Each time Charles clapped his hand to his forehead and said, darn it, he'd forgotten it.

What he was doing, in fact, was stacking the biscuit tins under his bed at the naval depot, complete with their consignments of cakes too tough to eat. He couldn't think what to do with them, and while he was waiting for inspiration the Admiral did a tour of inspection one day and asked what in thunder he had in all those tins. Charles said cakes. 'Cakes!' roared the Admiral incredulously. 'Don't you share 'em out with your friends?'

Charles explained. 'Sounds as if they'd be useful against the Luftwaffe,' said the Admiral, 'but heaven knows what they'd do to the guns. Dump 'em boy. Tell your girl friend it's an order. AND GET RID OF THOSE BLASTED TINS!'

That was the end of my cake-making sessions. Charles couldn't risk it happening again. When he came home he explained the situation tactfully, assuring me that he'd intended to eat them but somehow they'd mounted up and the Old Man had this thing about tins... I didn't mind. I didn't much like cooking anyway. I preferred to spend the weekends when he didn't come home writing him extra letters. So everybody was happy and the months went by while Charles completed his training.

It seems adventurous now. We were young, and instead of life as it would have been but for the war — uneventful office days, tennis in the evenings, dances, getting engaged, a wedding with the date fixed a year ahead — there we were in a whirl of uniforms, partings, homecomings, people marrying at the drop of a hat, get-togethers of friends home on leave who knew only too well that they might never meet again.

I remember going with Charles, his brother and some of their friends to a party one night at a pub. There was a time when my grandmother would have had the vapours at the idea of my entering such a place, but the war and Charles had changed all that. It sounds corny now. We sang 'There'll always be an England' while a couple of Somerset Yeomanry goose-stepped exaggeratedly round the floor. We were in an upstairs room: the landlord kept it specially for Forces parties and the drinks and food came up in a service lift.

There was a fighter pilot there with moustaches like Texas steer horns and a striped woollen scarf wound round and round his neck. He was cocooned in it like a Michelin tyre advertisement, and even then the ends dangled down to the floor. Two of his friends solemnly unwound him from it, revolving him like a top. They sat him in the lift, shouted, 'Chocks away,' somebody pulled the rope and the lift went down. Up it came again moments later, the pilot holding a pint of beer in either hand. They hauled him out, re-wound him into his scarf, and hoisted him shoulder high still clutching the beer. Charles's brother said it was a ritual whenever Pete came home. I can hear us laughing and applauding him now. And see the numbness in his eyes.

We came out afterwards to the beginning of an air-raid. The siren was just tailing down. It was a moonlight night, the stars were out, wispy clouds were scudding across the sky. High above us, in the silence before the guns started up, we could hear the unmistakable brooom-pause-brooom of a German bomber. The searchlights were hunting for it, criss-crossing the sky. The gun in the park behind us started firing. And just as we heard the first bomb come down, Charles dropped the distributor cover.

He and his brother had borrowed their mother's car: she saved her petrol ration for their leaves. By this time cars had to be immobilised at night, this being one of the dottier wartime rulings. I can't really believe, if we'd had a night invasion, that the invaders would have run round looking for private cars. Most of them had been laid up for the duration, anyway, and the petrol in the rest wouldn't have got the enemy far.

Anyway, the rule was that you disconnected the battery or removed the distributor cap. Charles had done the latter. And in trying to replace it in the dark without a torch—which you weren't allowed to use in an air-raid in case the Germans saw it (how they could distinguish a torch-beam with all those searchlights about, or why they should immediately aim a bomb at it if they did, was another of the war's imponderables)—in trying to replace it he'd dropped it. It went right down through the engine, and there we were: completely stranded.

If anyone had told me a year before that I would stand by a car in an air-raid without turning a hair while Charles and his brother lay on their stomachs looking for the distributor cap with matches (the idea being that the enemy could hardly spot match-flames, which anyway were underneath the car), while I kept an eye open for passing air-raid wardens... if anyone had told me that, I'd have said they were potty. It just shows what one can get used to.

I remember watching an aerial dog-fight out of the office window: the combatants soaring, twisting, diving with machine-guns firing, the German plane with its black wing-crosses eventually plummetting down, smoke pouring from its tail, while the Spitfire barrel-rolled across the sky in victory.

I remember my grandmother, one Saturday morning, coming back from shopping in the High Street mad as a hatter because a German plane, driven off from a daylight raid on an aircraft factory, had dropped its load of bombs at random. One had landed in the High Street, fortunately killing nobody, but a piece of shrapnel had gone clean through a nearby car. She didn't give a thought that it might have gone clean through her. Grandma, who'd been born before cars were even invented. Who'd gone round the Horn in a sailing ship when she was two, when the only things in the sky were stars. Herring Hitler was making a mistake, she said. (Like Churchill, she always mispronounced the names

of people she didn't like.) He wasn't going to frighten *her*. Somebody who saw the incident told us later that she didn't flinch an inch. She just looked up at the sky and glared.

I remember hearing church bells ringing in the distance at three o'clock one morning, heralding, so we thought, the expected invasion. What had really happened was that a German bomber had been hit and the crew had parachuted out. They were rounded up by farm-workers with pitchforks but, seeing them floating down, the local Home Guard commander had taken them for paratroops and had had the church bells rung, this being the prearranged invasion warning. Other than this, the bells were silent throughout the war.

It was hours before the news got through to us that it was a false alarm. We rather wondered when our own bells didn't ring, but my grandmother said that didn't mean anything. Our vicar was such a muddler he'd probably mislaid the key to the tower, or the Germans had got there before he did.

That was a thought. I remember peering out at the dawn-dim street imagining coal-scuttle helmets appearing in it at any moment. I remember, too, pondering what to do if the Germans had really landed. Grandma and Louisa would be as all right as possible. They had Great-Uncle William to look after them. But Charles was still in England, on the South coast. Could I somehow get to join him? If we were cut off... if he was sent to Germany as a prisoner... we might never see each other again. It *couldn't* happen. I wouldn't let it. Somehow I would manage to find him.

It sounds exciting now. But it wasn't like that at the time. I only remember feeling cheated that we couldn't have the normal, see-each-other-every-evening type of courtship that Louisa's generation had enjoyed.

The Germans didn't come, though. Grandma said they didn't dare, knowing what was waiting for them if they did. In her case it was the poker, which she kept ready by her bed.

The invasion scare passed, leave was resumed, Charles came home again. It was late September now, the tail-end of the Battle of Britain. I remember going with Charles and his brother, who was home on sick leave from the R.A.F., for a day's fishing on Stourton Lake. It was a glorious day, warm and mellow, and full of the drowsy peacefulness that presages autumn. Apples hung red in the Wiltshire orchards; dahlias and sunflowers crammed the cottage gardens with colour; smoke rose darkly on the horizon... I thought it was a farmer burning stubble.

It wasn't. It was a burning German plane. We saw three more shot down. Spitfires zoomed round them like hornets attacking hawks—hunters coming in for the kill. The end of the Battle of Britain. It didn't seem particularly remarkable then. We drove on to Stourton, hired a boat, and Charles and his brother fished peacefully all day.

I did most of the rowing. Charles's brother couldn't, being convalescent, and as Charles said, he couldn't row *and* fish. Twice he cast into an overhanging tree. It took some doing, manoeuvring the boat and holding it steady while Charles swayed and wobbled in the bows, standing up to unhitch the hook and nearly tipping us all into the water.

It was dusk when at last we drove back to town with a dozen fish in the creel. Across a couple of fields the wreckage of one of the German planes

was still smouldering. Sightseers had arrived now. Cars and bicycles were parked along the road, their owners scattered over the landscape souvenir-hunting. This morning the crew of that plane had been young and alive, like us. I hoped they had survived. I wished the war could be over and Charles and I living the life we'd planned, in the country. It didn't strike me that war was exciting.

Chapter Five

We'd won that round but the war still had years to run, and in December Charles came home on embarkation leave. He hadn't been told his destination but he'd been issued with tropical kit, which could mean the Middle East, India or maybe China. Wherever it was, he would be a long time away. Foreign drafts in the Navy were for two-and-a-half years. There was no coming home in the middle.

He knocked at the door one Friday night, having walked from the station in an air-raid. Grandma, Louisa and I were sheltering under the stairs. Great-Uncle William was in the garden watching for fire-bombs. I knew as soon as I heard his knock that it was Charles, though I hadn't expected him that weekend. I let him in and he told me his news. We sat on the stairs and decided to get married. If we had to spend the next two-and-a-half years apart, it would help to know we belonged.

We were married by licence on Monday afternoon. There was no time for special preparations. No time to arrange for guests, a trousseau or a reception: in fact we only just made it to the wedding. Living in a cathedral town, we could get a licence and be married the same day. We applied at the diocesan office on Monday morning. 'St Paul's?'

said the official when we told him where we wanted to be married. 'Wasn't that one bombed in last night's raid? You'd better go and make sure it's still standing.'

There were no telephones. They'd been put out of order the previous night. There weren't any buses either. We had to walk by a circuitous route through streets pitted with bomb-craters, picking our way round avalanches of rubble, held up for ages at a barricade while firemen pulled down a dangerously leaning warehouse front, hauling on it with a rope like a tug-of-war team, with Charles lending a hand on the end. The warehouse was near the river. I'd known it all my life. I used to ride past it with my grandmother on the open-topped trams, before they replaced them with buses. It was built like a fortress with great stone lintels over the windows and a massive oak door that was barred with iron. I little thought to see it pulled down on my wedding day. It had looked as if it was there for ever.

The church was still standing, though. The vicar was sweeping up broken glass but he was open, he said, for business. We trudged back across the bomb-wastes like explorers headed for the Pole, armed with the information. 'Gosh, we certainly were keen, weren't we?' said Charles when I reminded him of it not long ago. The diocesan registrar filled in the forms and told us to be back at two for the swearing-in of the licence. The Archdeacon wouldn't be there till then, he said: we'd arranged with the vicar to marry us at four. Bags of time, we thought. It was now eleven-thirty. We'd forgotten about the walking.

Back to my grandmother's to tell her what was happening and instruct Louisa to be at the church at four. On to Charles's mother, who lived on the edge of town, a good three miles away. She couldn't walk that distance and she couldn't use her car, with the roads roped off and bomb-pitted as they were, but we had a hasty lunch with her, she kissed us and we started out again. Back to the diocesan office to have the licence sworn in; to a jeweller's for the ring, which we bought at three. Back across the river to my grandmother's for my best kid gloves, which I couldn't find, then a sprint to the church, which we reached with minutes to spare.

If we hadn't been there by four we couldn't have been married till next day. Those were the church regulations. The vicar and the verger were looking at their watches, Louisa was waiting patiently. Dear Louisa, there when she was wanted, as she had been all my life. 'Have you got my gloves?' I whispered. Sure enough, she had borrowed them. She exchanged them for my winter mitts, I panted up the aisle, and so Charles and I were married.

My grandmother wasn't there. She kept her rule about not going to weddings, even when it was mine. She hadn't gone to any of her sons', she said: she wasn't going to alter her custom now.

I knew what it was. She had loved me so much she couldn't bear to witness my leaving her legally, even for Charles, whom she adored. So she stayed at home and got a meal for us, and Louisa produced a bottle of sherry. At least, we thought it was sherry. It was clear and golden and Louisa poured us large glasses. She'd given us too much, we protested. 'Nonsense,' said Louisa, 'This is your wedding day. Lift your glasses and drink up!'

We did. She'd given us neat whisky. We had to bang each other on the back to get our breath. She didn't know it would do *that*, said Louisa, who had never tasted whisky in her life. Apparently she'd gone into a wine merchants at lunchtime, explained about our getting married, asked the owner if he could spare a bottle of sherry and, though he didn't know her from Adam, he'd let her have a bottle of whisky. She had that effect on people. Everybody liked her. One day it would be her *downfall*, Grandma told her severely. Not knowing whisky would do that, indeed. Sometimes she despaired of Louisa. Supposing he'd plied her with it in the shop and we hadn't even known she was there?

We had difficulty in working out that one. Even watered, the whisky was pretty strong. When we left at seven to go up to Charles's parents, we were walking on air in more ways than one. We'd certainly had a wedding day to remember, said Charles . . . but it wasn't over yet. We had two days left for a honeymoon. We didn't want to spend it in town, so we packed a bag and from Charles's parents' house we caught the last country-bound bus at nine o'clock. The country buses were still running: it was only in town that they'd been temporarily stopped.

Where were we going? We didn't know. Only that we were married, together, and on a bus. In two days time we would be separated for years . . . but that was the day after tomorrow. It was a Bridgwater bus. It would pass through Enna's village. I'd suddenly remembered, I told Charles. About two miles this side of Enna's on the main road, was an old Georgian coaching hotel.

We got off outside it. I can see us now, going up the drive to the pillared porch. Somewhat wearily. We'd had quite a day, what with the walking and the whisky and all the excitement.

I can see the door opening, a woman looking out, and Charles saying we would like a room. 'Sorry, we're full up,' she said. 'With all these air-raids in town, everybody's coming out here to sleep.' She suggested we try the inn along the road. They were full up, too. We couldn't have phoned ahead because of the telephones being out of order, but in any case we hadn't expected this.

'Ask the air-raid warden,' one of the pub customers called out. 'He knows everybody round here who has rooms.' An air-raid warden out here, miles from town? What on earth did he do? we wondered. A spare room in a cottage wasn't exactly the honeymoon inn we'd envisaged, either, but there was a war on: we had to sleep somewhere.

What the warden did was made clear to us when we located his bungalow, with its AIR-RAID WARDEN plate on the gate. Go to bed early was what *he* did — presumably in case he ever did have to get up. It was not yet ten o'clock, but when we knocked on the door one of the bungalow windows opened and a figure in a nightshirt looked out. 'You woke us up,' he said. He was minus his teeth. I remember thinking what a recommendation for marriage.

No, he said, he didn't know of a room. Every one was taken hereabouts. People were bringing blankets and sleeping on the floor in the village hall. Did we have any blankets? We hadn't. Nor any inclination to spend our wedding night on the floor of the village hall. We thanked him politely and left.

I was standing in the road doing what I was to do so often in the years ahead — wail 'Why does it have to happen to us!' — when a burly figure materialised out of the darkness and said he wondered if he could help. He was a farmer and his wife took in guests. They were pretty full, but they did have one room spare. He'd heard us asking in the pub... he'd been in the middle of a game of shove-ha'penny and couldn't break off then, but he'd come after us as soon as he'd finished.

He had his van in the pub yard. He drove us to the farm, which was just as well, since I was practically on my knees. The other guests were having coffee and biscuits in the sitting-room and we were invited to join them. I remember oak beams, polished brass, chintz-covered armchairs, a log fire with two Labradors stretched out in front of it... somebody asking whether we'd come out to get away from the blitz and my replying yes. My husband, I said, was on embarkation leave: we'd felt like a few days' peace. I laid my hand on my chair arm, displaying my wedding ring. I didn't want them to think we weren't married. It was so obviously new, of course, that was probably just what they did think. Honestly, I never could win. All the more so when we were shown to our room and I looked at myself in the mirror — at the bomb-dust that coated my hair like powder (I never wore a hat), at the streak of dirt, like Indian paint on my cheek. I looked as if Charles had found me in the gutter. Really, I said, he might have *told* me. Charles said he'd been too darned busy all day to notice.

It was a lovely old room: cream-washed walls, dark oak beams, shaded lamps casting reflections on the low, sloping ceiling. And when I woke in the morning — arriving in the dark I hadn't realised quite where we were — there, through the window, was Dolbury Hill with the ramparts on it, where I had walked so often with Louisa and Enna.

Tom, Enna's husband, said afterwards that if he'd known we were there he'd have been over with some of his pals to bang the buckets for us. It was just as well he didn't know. The other guests would probably have had a fit and have roused the toothless air-raid warden thinking the invasion had really started.

As it was, we had our two days' honeymoon in peace, then it was time to see Charles off at the station. More walking — his train left at 6.30 in the morning — but I was able to get a bus back to my grandmother's afterwards. 'Keep the ticket, dear,' said the conductress. 'It's a return if it's issued before half-past eight: you can use it again tonight.' I nearly said it would be two-and-a-half years before I needed a ticket for the return journey on that bus. But I didn't. It was my private affair. I got off and went home to my grandmother.

Who said she'd been thinking: I ought to get a bike. Louisa must have one as well. Then we could go for rides in the country. It would keep me from moping and I could keep an eye open for that cottage we wanted. She'd heard you could still buy eggs in the country, too, if you knew the right place to go. There was that nice farmer she used to buy butter from in the market. Where was it he lived? Somewhere out around Axbridge? She was sure he'd let us have eggs. We could buy vegetables, too — cabbages and things — they'd be cheaper and fresher straight from the country.

We got our bikes. It was a marvellous idea of my grandmother's. Riding round the countryside cheered me up no end. But we never got to her farmer friend at Axbridge, which was eighteen miles away. We made the attempt a couple of times but it wasn't any use. Louisa either got winded before we got there or fell off.

She was in her middle thirties now — no age at all, but the trouble was she hadn't ridden a bike for years. The one she'd had in Harold's day had been one of the ladies' upright variety that she'd sailed slowly along on as if she was on a penny-farthing. Even then it had been too much for her. She'd been coming down a hill one day — probably doing about four miles an hour: Louisa never went very fast — when, feeling the bike begin to speed up, she'd put on her brakes: the front ones instead of the back. She'd gone over the handlebars, lost her nerve, and hadn't ridden since. It didn't help, now that Grandma insisted she should, to find that bikes had altered considerably in the interim.

They were lower, sturdier—the ladies' models were exactly like the men's, only without a crossbar—and they lacked the accommodating curve in front through which Louisa was accustomed to put her foot. In the days when you braked gently some way before you actually stopped, that was, and, with your left foot still on the pedal, brought your right foot through in front of it, glided elegantly poised on the pedal for the last few yards and, when you finally touched down on the pavement, executed a few dainty little running steps to show what an accomplished young lady you were.

The modern bikes were shorter and the bracing bar was straight, not curved. Louisa was forever catching her toe in it, trying to do the gliding bit. We'd had the bicycles for a good six months before we went on our cycling tour. We had the same fortnight's holiday from our jobs but my grandmother wouldn't hear of coming away with us. She couldn't leave the house in wartime, she said: if she did, that was just when that Herring Hitler or Marshal Gloring *would* come, and William would let the Nasties in without a word and goodness knew what would happen to the animals. So we decided to do a cycling tour up the Wye Valley. Only for a week out of our fortnight. Grandma's nerves wouldn't have stood it if she'd had to worry about us for longer than that.

We set out for the Aust Ferry. This was before they built the Severn Bridge. It was August and we hadn't gone far before, naturally, it began to rain in the good old English summer fashion. We had our clothing coupons with us so we bought ourselves cycling capes and sou'-westers. Nothing was going to stop us. Mine was yellow, Louisa's was pillar-box red. We certainly looked professional, cycling in single file up the Gloucester Road: Louisa, as usual, in the rear.

As I neared the bottom of the hill leading down to the ferry, I looked back over my shoulder. That was usual too. Louisa, remembering her mishap with her previous bike, not only proceeded downhill even slower than she cycled on the flat: if it was very steep she got off and walked.

Sure enough she was a considerable way behind, obviously about to alight. I got off myself to wait for her, keeping my head turned back. As I watched, Louisa, who was apparently completely stationary, fell off that bike before my very eyes. How could she do it when she was *stopped*? I demanded, rushing back to pick her up. Easily. With a cycling cape fore and aft over the bike, with Louisa it was inevitable.

It rained and rained. Remembering to shout back at her to watch her cape every time she got off was only one of the journey's trials. My grandmother had packed some food for us: sandwiches and a large tart, which were in Louisa's cycle basket when she fell off. We picked them up. There were no plastic bags in those days. What with the rain and hitting the road they were all soggy. On the other side of the ferry we ate the sandwiches but we couldn't eat the tart — there was jam oozing out of it all over. It was blackcurrant jam and it had turned the pastry grey. The tart was also incredibly heavy. It wasn't just its being waterlogged. It had been like that to start with. Grandma wasn't the world's best pastry-maker and the flour wasn't very good in wartime. I suggested we left it in the hedge for some hard-pressed animal. Louisa was absolutely aghast. Waste food in wartime? she said. We must take it with us. Somebody would be glad to have it.

It was just my luck. If it had been fine we might have come across some children playing or a deserving tramp pushing his belongings on a pram. But it had to be raining and, pushing up the hill to Chepstow, Louisa had to discover that her handlebars were bent. It must have happened when she fell off, she said. She'd have to find a garage. She did. The biggest garage in Chepstow where, it being a slow-moving afternoon in wartime, not only did they straighten Louisa's handlebars where they would normally only deal with cars, but two apprentices and the foreman gathered round to do it.

The foreman refused to charge anything for such a small job. The apprentices were fourteen-year-olds and skinny. I could see Louisa casting about for some reward, and her eyes alighted on the basket. 'You can't!' I hissed, going hot and cold all over. She did though. She gave them the squashed jam tart to have with their tea, presenting it as if she were a duchess.

They stood there in a group as we wheeled our bicycles

out through the door, the foreman in the middle holding the sticky package. Embarrassed to the tips of my toes, I couldn't wait to get out of sight round the corner. Honestly, I said . . . how on earth she had the nerve . . . Nonsense, said Louisa airily. She'd had five brothers. She remembered their appetites. Men *liked* their pastry stodgy.

In our house they had to, that was the only way they got it, but that was typical of Louisa. She was either like this — full of supreme self-confidence, as she'd been about the ragwort and the harvest festival — or stark with unreasoning nervousness, as when she saw a cow or went downhill on her bicycle.

She was still full of confidence when we reached St Briavels. Maybe it was being away from Grandma's jurisdiction. Anyway, when we asked at a guest house whether they could put us up for the night and the proprietress told us she had only one small single vacant . . . but, she said, on second thoughts one of her regulars *was* away for a couple of nights . . . he was an Air Force officer and he'd gone away on business . . . she didn't like to turn us away in this dreadful weather . . . maybe one of us could have *his* room . . . it was Louisa who announced decisively that she would have it. 'My niece,' she said, 'will take the little one.'

It was Louisa, therefore, who had a traumatic experience during the night, when the Air Force officer arrived back ahead of time (being a resident he had his own latch-key), crept quietly upstairs so as not to disturb anybody, went into his room and found our heroine in his bed.

'What are you doing in *my* bed?' he demanded. Explanations followed in the dark: they couldn't put the light on because of the blackout. Being a gentleman, he then retired to sleep downstairs on a settee while Louisa put a chair against the door.

I knew nothing of this till the morning. Actually Louisa took it very well, though her self-confidence was obviously shaken. Was this what happened when one went out into the world? I could see her thinking. You found yourself in strange men's beds?

It was a different Louisa who walked round the ruins of Tintern Abbey. She wouldn't have pressed a jam tart on anyone there. It was a different Louisa who climbed with me to the top of Symond's Yat, dead scared of going too near the edge. We shared a bedroom that night at a cottage near Monmouth. Louisa wasn't taking any chances. The floor was warm from being over the Aga: we dried our wet clothes on it. It was a big room, with a sloping floor and dormer windows. Fun, wasn't it? I said. And had she noticed the rose growing round the privy door? I reckoned it was the same rose they had at Enna's. I wouldn't mind a cottage like this. She wouldn't, said Louisa. Could I help her pull the washstand across the door? She wished we were home with Grandma.

After that it only needed an encounter with a bull to bring our cycling tour to an end. We were heading for Ross-on-Wye by way of the side-lanes because there were Army convoys on the main road and Louisa, flustered by the noise when they rumbled past, had kept getting off for them. I had to use a map to find our way along the side-lanes. People were suspicious of strangers with maps in wartime, but they'd removed all the country signposts when they were expecting the invasion and I couldn't find Ross-on-Wye without one.

So there I was, expecting to be arrested at any moment, Louisa cycling slowly along behind me, when suddenly on a steep-sloping hillock ahead of us on the right, I saw this enormous bull: a massive Hereford, standing imposingly under a tree and looking straight towards us. Oh well, I thought, it *must* be in a field and the field, though I couldn't see one, must have a fence. It hadn't, though. As I got nearer I could see that at the foot of the hillock, separating it from the road, there was only a very low, recently cut-down hedge.

Crumbs, I thought, thinking of the cow jumping over the moon. I bet that bull could easily clear that lot. It was no good turning back, though. That *could* bring him charging after us. Just keep cycling steadily past, that was the ticket ... I seemed to be cycling on the spot for ages, never getting any nearer, but gradually I drew level with the bull—at which point I realised with relief that it was tethered, fastened to the tree with a heavy chain. At which same point, inevitably, Louisa looked up from pedalling behind me with her eyes fixed on the road, spotted the bull for the first time and fell off.

She practically passed out this time. As it was, she refused absolutely to go past. There might be others, she said, or this one might get loose and come after us. We would have to go back to the main road.

So we went back round the corner, and I consulted the map: there was nothing for it but to retrace our steps. Back to the main road, the convoys swishing past us, Louisa getting off every time they did. I didn't know about her, I said, when we got to Ross-on-Wye, but somehow it didn't seem the right weather for a cycle tour. What did she say to our cutting it short, heading straight for Gloucester, putting our bikes on the train and going home?

So it was that, two days after we'd started out, we opened the back door of our house in Bristol and pushed our bicycles through. My grandmother was sitting on the garden seat. She hadn't expected us back for another five days. I can still see the look on her face when she saw us — as if Christmas had come in August. 'Thank goodness,' she said. 'If you two went away for good I'd have to leave home myself.'

It was nice to know she'd missed us. Great-Uncle William it seemed, hadn't been much help. Missing us himself, he'd spent two days and evenings mooning round the garden and had sprayed the Grow for Victory lettuces practically out of existence.

Chapter Six

We didn't do any more cycle tours. I don't think my nerves would have stood it. Grandma had a fit when she heard about the guest house anyway and said it wasn't safe to let Louisa out of her sight. Half a day away from home and there she was getting into a strange man's bed. Did she realise she might have been *murdered*?

Louisa hadn't until then but she did after that. She didn't suggest another tour. We rode out to Enna's one Saturday for the weekend, but there was a heavy raid that night on Bristol. We could hear the bombers going over in wave after wave as we lay in bed in the cottage. We were safe enough, but what about Grandma back in town? We could hear the gunfire and the crump of the bombs in the distance.

We went home next morning — I have never seen Louisa ride so fast: she didn't even get off going down the hills — to find that a bomb had dropped in the road but our house had escaped, though all the windows were out. Grandma was safe. She'd been in the cupboard under the stairs with Baldwin, the

dog, Macdonald, the cat, and Snowden and Piquita, her parrots. Great-Uncle William was safe, too, though somewhat deaf. ('Deafer,' commented Grandma, 'than usual.') He'd been blown back through the kitchen door when the bomb landed and the blast had temporarily affected his eardrums. 'Got one advantage,' he confided to Louisa. 'I can't hear a word your mother says.'

Nothing was going to get those two down, but we couldn't leave them on their own again. So our cycling was confined to the near-radius of town and I didn't find Charles's and my dream cottage. Everything with a roof on it was occupied by people getting out of town at night away from the air-raids, anyway. There wouldn't be any vacant cottages until after the war.

I wrote to Charles about our adventures. He couldn't tell me of his because of censorship. I only knew he was based somewhere in Egypt. He wrote of how, when they were off duty and not being bombed by Rommel, he and his friend Simmy used to sit outside their tent at night, drinking coffee which they'd brewed, looking at the moon shining over the desert and wondering if I was looking at it in England. Really poetic, it was. And Charles brewing the coffee... I imagined him doing it one day in a home of our own. It wasn't until he was back in England that I discovered it was Simmy who brewed the coffee. Charles did the looking at the moon.

Meanwhile, while he was overseas, I joined the Red Cross, working during the day at my office job, which was scheduled as essential, and at the hospital in the evenings and at weekends. Louisa, who had dropped Esperanto for a while, now took it up again. I don't know whether she had visions of becoming an interpreter when the Allies invaded Europe, but I remember one vignette of home life at that period.

I'd just completed the fifty hours' intensive training which was a requisite of wartime V.A.D. work and which included watching an operation. We were having supper and I was recounting the details of the hernia op I'd seen, extremely proud of the fact that I hadn't fainted. Many would-be V.A.D.s did: some of them folded up the moment they saw a hypodermic syringe. I remember a lecture on giving injections when they were carried out in shoals. Anyway, I was describing the details, Grandma was listening enthralled, interposing her reminiscences of when her youngest son, my Uncle Lester, had had his tonsils out before the First World War.

Things were primitive in those days, she said. They'd given him too much anaesthetic and had to lay him out in the snow to get him round. She could see it as if it were yesterday, his wan little face in the hospital yard and the blood all over the snow . . . Louisa at her end of the table was meanwhile reciting loudly '*En la gardeno estas ronda tablo*', probably so she couldn't hear what we were saying, her stomach being somewhat delicate. 'God Almighty,' roared Great-Uncle William, slamming down his knife and fork. 'That man Hitler's got something to answer for. He ought to be made to be *here* (banging the table), eating *Spam* (banging his plate), and having to listen to this lot.'

So we continued . . . Sharing our hardships, said Grandma: working for Victory, patiently content with our meagre rations . . . She only slipped from the path of virtue once. When Enna wrote to say her Uncle Walter was killing a pig, officially for his own consumption, but there was only him and Aunt Allie and if Grandma would like a ham . . . provided, of course, she kept mum. Grandma would. She'd always fancied curing a ham but had never known where to get one raw. There was also, now, the added incentive that we weren't half fed up with Spam. Just one ham, said Grandma. She didn't think Mr Churchill would mind. After all, where did *he* get all his brandy?

So the plot was set in motion. The pig was to be killed. Enna was to bring the ham to town on the bus. She was to get off at a bus-stop on the outskirts, where I would meet her, hand me the ham, then cross to the bus-stop on the

other side of the road, where she would get the same bus on its return journey in twenty minutes' time and head straight back for the country. Why she couldn't have come to our house and had an hour or two's visit — or at least come right into the bus depot, where I could have met her equally well and, if she *had* to go straight back, she could have just sat in the bus while it turned round — I haven't a clue. I was young and didn't ask questions. Maybe it was some cloak-and-dagger action, either as practised in rural black markets, or specially thought up by Grandma.

I only know that, as I waited for Enna to descend from the bus, took charge of the ham, exchanged a brief word, watched her cross the road and then, lugging the contraband in its suitcase, started my own journey home, I expected to be apprehended at any moment. I would never have made a secret agent.

It was all for nothing, anyway. Grandma worked on that ham for a fortnight, rubbing it with saltpetre, soaking it in brine, turning it religiously every day. At the end of that time it had turned quite green and Great-Uncle William said either the ham left home or he did. It was beginning to smell as though we had something wrong with the drains. Grandma, when at last she admitted defeat, said it wasn't Enna's fault: she'd only brought it in on the bus. But if she could lay hands on that old rogue Walter... Five pounds she'd paid for that ham, and he'd probably had it in an outhouse for several days before he'd sent it up. She hadn't liked him much when she'd seen him at Mrs Wilson's. Always with his feet in a bowl. Probably where he kept the ham, said Great-Uncle William, who was hardly renowned for his tact.

So two-and-a-half years passed and suddenly Charles was on his way home. I could hardly believe that at last it was actually happening. It was an anxious time: there was

no news at all for six weeks while the convoy came home via the Cape, zig-zagging wide across the Atlantic to avoid the submarine lanes, never safe from attack until it docked. Eventually a telegram arrived. A neighbour brought it down to my office. He was back. He would be on the six o'clock train. I walked to the station to meet him. No bus for me this time. I wanted to savour every minute of it.

After a month's home leave he was sent to London on a course and my firm transferred me to their London office so I could be with him. We lived out at Highgate. No frenzied wartime London for us. No Rainbow Corner or dancing at the Savoy. We walked on Hampstead Heath, went out to Epping Forest, watched the squirrels chasing up and down the trees, never imagining that in due course an orphan squirrel was to lead us to the cottage we'd dreamed of for so long.

It was a comparatively quiet time. The air raids had

lessened. The V-bombs hadn't yet started. It was August, and London's suburban gardens, geared to digging for victory, looked more like country allotments in their bounteousness. Runner beans hung like bananas from string tied up walls; marrows rioted over lush-looking compost heaps; onions, their tops turned over to indicate that their owners had reared them to full, triumphant growth, ripened like the domes of Brighton Pavilion. Tomatoes bore fruit against every garden fence. Fat round lettuces dotted the borders in front of them. Crammed in odd corners were dahlias, scarlet, purple and orange, and sunflowers the size of chimney-sweeping brushes. One couldn't eat those, but they were important too, as a symbol of London's intrepidness.

There was a harvest air about the Highgate gardens. It reminded me of the August long ago when I'd been taken to Enna's wedding and had first decided that I wanted to live in the country. It had the same effect on Charles. Egypt had nothing of this, he said. Gosh, if only the war would end. When *would* we get to the country?

Sooner than either of us imagined, actually. We could hardly believe our luck when, after Charles had finished his course in London, he was posted to a shore-station in the South West. In the heart of the country where, if he could find living-out quarters, I would be able to join him. It might be only for six months or so: shore postings were pretty transient in wartime. But it would be worth it — we'd been apart for two-and-a-half years — if we could find somewhere to stay.

Again we were in luck. Charles met someone who was being posted abroad and who had living-out quarters in a nearby village. His wife would be going back to her people when he went, he said. If Charles moved fast, he might get their rooms. Charles cycled to the village and saw the owner — an elderly widower who took to him at once — that very night. Undoubtedly it was the Maurice Chevalier air, which had such an effect on Grandma. 'If your Missis likes it,' said old Mr Chidley, 'I'll hold it till you can move in.'

He was a grand old boy. He kept it vacant for us for six weeks though he said he didn't like living in an empty house. I had to give a month's notice to my firm, however, and wait till the end of the month to do it, so it was impossible for us to move in before then. I'd gone down the weekend after Charles had first seen it, though, to see what I thought of it myself.

It was hardly the cottage of my dreams. It was a squat, double-fronted stone-built house in one of those rows that line the pavements of village streets. Once it had been a pub. It was still called King William House. You entered down a step, through a doorway in the centre, into a wide old flagstoned passage that ran to the back of the house.

First on our left was the former tap-room. 'Where,' Mr Chidley informed us, clattering over the flagstones in his boots, 'Mr and Mrs Thompson do live. I'll take 'ee in to see Mrs Thompson later.' First on the right was a tiny parlour, with a staircase in the corner spiralling up to the bedrooms.

Beyond the Thompsons' room on the left was what appeared to be a dungeon. According to Mr Chidley it was where they used to keep the beer. Obviously the equivalent of a cellar, it was stone-floored, stone-walled and had a high-up window about a foot square. It now held a meat-safe, two jugs of milk on a wide stone bench — Mr Chidley said this was where they used to keep the barrels — and two frying-pans hanging side by side on the wall. His and Mrs Thompson's.

Beyond the parlour on the right was another stone-walled room. Goodness knows what they used to keep in there. It now had a roof-light and contained two heaps of coal in separate corners, an oil-stove on a table and Mrs Thompson's bike. 'I lights the range in the kitchen about eight o'clock,' Mr Chidley explained, 'and Mrs Thompson cooks on that all day. But for getting Mr Thompson off to the camp early in the morning, she do use this stove out here.'

I would have to, too. Well, what did it matter? Enna had cooked on an oil-stove and she'd managed pretty well. We clattered on out to the kitchen, which was very like Enna's mother's: large, low-ceilinged, with a fire burning in a range and an enormous fringed-clothed table in the centre. A fringed-clothed mantelpiece, too, with the usual conglomeration on it: china dogs, brass candlesticks, paper spills in a blue and white jug. A Victorian sideboard against the wall. Ordinary-sized, though, not like Mrs Martin's. Rag rugs on the flagstoned floor, the one in front of the fire occupied by a stretched-out-flat white terrier. On one side of the fire was a high-backed wooden armchair with an old red cushion and a cat on it. There was a battery wireless on the window-seat, a calendar with a pocket on the wall, Mrs Chidley's cap on a hook behind the door and a big black kettle on the hob.

There was also electric light, Mr Chidley pointed out proudly. Mr Thompson was an engineer and he'd put it in quite recently. Only in their sitting room and in Mr Chidley's kitchen. Mr Chidley wouldn't have it anywhere else. People only walked through the parlour to get to the stairs, he said, and what did you want with it in bedrooms?

We returned to the front of the house and he tapped on the Thompsons' door. Mrs Thompson was sewing in front of the fire. I wished afterwards that I'd taken more notice of her, since we were to hear her name so much. We were with Mr Chidley for more than a year and every disaster that happened during that time—the knob coming off the bottom of a claw-foot table (actually due to dry-rot); a door falling off a sideboard; the time when I poked holes right through a saucepan; the time when a chair went through the floor—all these, according to him, were a legacy of Mrs Thompson's stay there. She wun't careful with things, he said.

At the time, though, I was too busy looking round our prospective sitting-room: small, with a little brass-fendered black grate, green and yellow linoleum on the floor, the three-clawed Victorian table destined to lose its knob, the sideboard destined to lose its door, a horsehair armchair, a horsehair sofa — the sort they upholster in velvet nowadays and charge a fortune for. There was a cupboard in the wall: it had once been the serving hatch through from the beer room, but it had been fitted with a false wooden back. It now held a supply of crockery, none of which appeared to match. (Mrs Thompson's fault, Mr Chidley confided to us later. It just came apart in her hands.)

We inspected the bedroom: lino-floored with a brass-railed bed and a dressing table, and a wash-stand with china appurtenances. (There was no bathroom, of course, but in the scullery beyond the kitchen I'd noticed a tin bath on the wall and a copper for heating the water.)

I looked through the bedroom window. On the opposite side of the road, over a high stone wall, was a farmyard in which a man was walking round and round in circles, obviously not realising he was visible to us. 'Thass Farmer Bennett,' observed Mr Chidley. 'Bin out in his outhouse drinkin' cider. Probably had a row with his wife. Then he got to walk round like that soberin' hisself up afore she'll let him in again.'

He put his nose closer to the window. 'Thass Mrs Charleycott down there,' he said. (Her name, we later discovered, was really Chaldicote, but she was always Mrs Charleycott to us.) 'I plays cards with she every night.' I peered down to see his lady friend. She was just entering her own front door, two houses up. He tapped on the glass. She looked up and wiggled her fingers. He wiggled his fingers back. She was as fat as a Christmas pudding. I guessed rationing hadn't applied much to her. 'Fine woman', said Mr Chidley. I had to agree that she was.

I wandered over to the mantelpiece and looked at its

inevitable ornaments: two china shoes, the ubiquitous pin-cushion, a man and woman in old-fashioned clothes. I looked closer. One was Mr Pickwick, complete with wire-framed spectacles and a curly-brimmed hat. Wire spectacles on a china image? I looked at his companion. She had them too, together with an Empire-style dress and a bonnet, though she was too slim to be meant to be Mrs Bardell. I have never seen anything like it anywhere else. It must have been a Victorian china designer's idea of fun. Perfectly-formed pairs of spectacles, barely an inch wide, fitted to both china figures. What was even more amazing was that the figure of the woman had been broken and fitted together again like miniature crazy paving—even the face was in several pieces. But there it was, stuck together and the spectacles neatly replaced. It was a trait we were to become familiar with where Mr Chidley was concerned. He never threw anything away. Even when I poked the holes through the saucepan and replaced it, after considerable searching, with another (you could see daylight through the old one in about a dozen places and I'd dumped it in a dustbin in town), he said I shouldn't have thrown the old one away. He could have mended it with them pot-repairers. These were those tin and rubber arrangements, about the size of a sink plug, people used to fit either side of holes in pots. One, maybe, in those days of bleak austerity, but a *dozen* in a seven-inch enamel saucepan?

That is jumping ahead again, however. Mrs Thompson had broken the ornament, he informed me now. Terrible butter-fingered she was.

I didn't mind. The place was spotlessly clean. It had character even if it did appear to be disintegrating. We were lucky to find somewhere where Charles and I could be together in wartime. I wanted to see more of Mrs Charleycott, too, and the farmer across the road. It reminded me of Enna's village. This was why I wanted to live in the country.

I liked it, I said. I liked little old Mr Chidley, too. He had obviously taken to us. 'Better see the privy before you do make up your mind,' he said, clattering ahead of us down the stairs and out into the garden. It was, of course, an earth-closet with a rose growing round the door.

Chapter Seven

There were earth-closets and earth-closets and Mr Chidley's was one of the superior kind. It was built on to the house for a start: you didn't have to trudge up the garden to it Excelsior-fashion in gumboots. Mr Chidley emptied it every day, so as earth closets went it was flower-fresh. There was also a length of wattle fencing facing it on top of the garden wall which afforded privacy to one's comings and goings.

'Put that up for Mrs Thompson,' Mr Chidley observed. 'She din't like the people next door seein' her come out.' I wouldn't either, I announced very firmly, in case he was thinking of taking it down now she was leaving. You never know with country people. They don't like wasting anything.

Take the way the medieval privy itself has survived down to modern times. Sir John Harington invented the water-closet in the reign of Elizabeth the First: she had one installed at Richmond and wrote him an enthusiastic letter about it. Four hundred years later, however, with modern plumbing universal in town and the septic tank system making it possible in rural districts where there was no main drainage, countrymen still clung like limpets to their earth-closets on account of the usefulness of the contents. On to their gardens it went, to help bring on the crops. Sometimes more precipitately than others. Mr Chidley, who had strong views on such matters, assured us that he tipped his into a pit. Left it there for a twelvemonth, he said, afore he dug it into the garden. Not like some folk as he could mention, who put it straight out round their veges. They might win all the prizes at the local shows but he 'ouldn't fancy eating *their* tomatoes.

Neither would we, and it was comforting, once we'd moved in, to know that he was so particular, since he insisted on providing us with home-grown vegetables which we couldn't have avoided eating. To a certain extent, at any rate... He would present me with a cauliflower, adjuring me not to waste the greens or stump, and watch me while I cooked it to see that I didn't. I would pile it dutifully into a tureen, take it into our sitting-room, and Charles and I would eat the florets. The remainder I would scrape into a newspaper, hide it in the sideboard, and when I went into the market town next day (being eligible for wartime work I'd been allocated to a job in the local Food Office) I would take the parcel with me and drop it in the bus station rubbish bin, feeling a positive traitor to my new role as a Food Office official.

Why didn't I put it in the dustbin at Mr Chidley's? Because Mr Chidley went through that with a toothcomb and was continually confronting me with what he'd found. A leather belt of Charles's from which the buckle had come

adrift: he could mend he with a liddle nut and bolt, he said. And he did. *And* Charles had no choice but to continue wearing it, until Mr Chidley got tired of examining it daily to see how it was holding, whereupon Charles discarded it at the double. Probably marked him for life, he said. That bolt had stuck into his stomach like a gimlet.

Likewise there was my umbrella, blasted inside-out one day by the wind that blew continually across the marshes and down the straight, flat street past King William House. Not for nothing had this been a Roman road: there wasn't a wind-deflecting bend in it between Rome and Bath. Two of the umbrella ribs were broken and as it was an old one I dumped it, too, in the dustbin, from which Mr Chidley promptly retrieved it and mended that with nuts and bolts as well. Unfortunately the nuts and bolts kept tangling up with the other ribs and the umbrella wouldn't shut down properly. Charles was lucky. He only had to wear his nut and bolted belt for a week or two before Mr Chidley turned his attention to other matters. My umbrella was more conspicuous. He saw it every time I took it out. I carried it for ages, one side of it drooping like the wing of an injured crow, before it occurred to me to leave it behind on the bus to town one morning. I came home that night with a new one. Mr Chidley voiced his disapproval. That umbrella should have lasted me for *years* now it was mended, he said. Careless I was, like all young people nowadays. He only hoped I'd never come to want for one.

As a matter of fact I needed an umbrella continuously while we lived in that village. It was early in the year when we moved in, and at first I thought it was just the season that caused it to rain as if we were working up to Noah's flood. For a time while we were there I kept a diary, which is not a normal habit of mine, but I kept one then for a few enthusiastic weeks and it makes evocative reading.

'Still raining,' says the entry for the third day after our arrival. 'Did washing. Took ration cards to butcher and grocer. Got wet. Wrote home for Wellingtons.'

'Washing not dry,' the saga continues next day. 'Visited butcher for sausages. Still raining. Cooked sausages and mashed potatoes (smoked) on Mr Chidley's range for supper. Wrote to town laundry, asking them to call as soon as possible.'

'Charles worried about his shirts' reads the following day's entry. 'Dried them in front of fire in desperation.' After which Charles was even more worried because I'd put them on an old-fashioned wooden towel-stand which I sneaked down from our bedroom (Mr Chidley not holding with clothes-horses); it was intended for damp towels, not sopping wet things, and the varnish came off on his uniform shirts. They dried with horizontal stripes, fortunately not where it showed, but did I realise, said Charles, the trouble he'd be in if the Captain spotted him wearing orange striped shirts?

What worried me was the trouble I'd be in if Mr Chidley found out about the towel-stand. Why *do* mishaps always happen with other people's possessions? There I was, knowing how he valued his, treating them as if they belonged in a museum, and this was the second catastrophe I'd achieved within our first week.

The first had been a few days previously when I'd caught the bedroom lino on fire. Again it had happened in all innocence. I wasn't being careless. My grandmother, concerned at the thought of my having to get up at six in the morning, before Charles went off to the camp, to make tea on the oil-stove in the former beer cellar (concerned though she might be, you notice she didn't expect Charles to do it), my grandmother, very helpfully, had bought me a spirit-lamp and kettle. Not the kind that stood on silver legs, complete with silver kettle, designed to grace an elegant Victorian tea-table. This was a wartime version: it looked like a round, flat-based brass pincushion, stood directly on the floor or whatever, and you poured the meths on to an asbestos pad in the middle. You lit it, and stood the Woolworth's tin kettle on the three black metal strips that formed a tripod above the flaming pot. It was the best she'd been able to find, said Grandma. It worked exactly the same as a proper one, anyway, and I'd be able to make the morning tea in our bedroom.

For two mornings I did, standing the stove in the black-leaded fireplace and crouching over it while it boiled, which took ages. To be fair, Charles did offer on both mornings to get out and watch it for me, then drifted blissfully back to his slumbers. My goodness it was cold. I bet that bedroom hadn't had a fire in it in its entire several hundred years, and Mr Chidley didn't have any oil-stoves for purely room heating. An oil-stove in the bedroom? Mrs Thompson had never asked for one of they, he said disapprovingly, when I timidly broached the subject. So for two mornings I made the tea on the ice-cold hearth and we drank it by candlelight in bed, Charles saying how cosy this was wasn't it, while I felt as if I'd just mushed back from the Arctic. And then I had a brainwave. I put the spirit-stove under the bed, together with teapot, milk and cups and saucers with the meths bottle standing by at the ready. All I had to do next morning was pull out the spirit-stove, pour on the meths, put it back on the floor beside the bed, light it, put the kettle on and then lie back and wait for it to boil without having to set foot out of the warmth of the bed.

Spirit-stoves, as I say, take a considerable time to boil. Long before it was time for the kettle to start singing I was aware of an acrid smell, as if someone was burning off paint. I looked over the edge of the bed. They certainly were. The bottom of the stove, heated by this time to the temperature of a flat-iron, had scorched the pattern off the lino, not only under the stove but for a good way round. Even by candlelight I could see the blisters.

'The floor's on fire,' I whispered to Charles, realising even in this extremity the need to deal with the matter quietly. Mr Chidley was asleep on the other side of the wall. Admittedly he was snoring like a traction engine, but there was a certain hesitation between the snores as if he was thinking of waking up at any moment. When, undoubtedly, the balloon would go up. Mrs Thompson wouldn't be in it. I could hear him telling his next lodgers — probably they wouldn't be long in succeeding either — how he'd had to be rescued by the fire brigade at six in the morning on account of my setting fire to the floor.

Charles, dependable as the Rock of Gibraltar in an emergency, was out of bed in a flash, flitting soundlessly round to my side of the bed, snatching up the washbasin jug as he came. 'Open the window *quietly*,' he whispered. That was to let out the smell. He dowsed the spirit-stove carefully — not too much water at a time on account of it hissed like a train letting off steam in a station. The lino cooled. Mr Chidley continued snoring. We decided against tea in bed in future. It still left me with the lino on my conscience, though. It was going to have to be explained some time.

Charles didn't worry about little things like that. They were all part of life, according to him. That was what he said when the next misfortune befell Mr Chidley's furnishings, as a result of our experimenting with table-turning. Charles's father had been interested in this. He used to tell us how, as a young man, he'd once seen a table get out of control and sail clean through a window. We'd tried it ourselves, on one of Charles's leaves, with Charles's brother and his fiancée. The table had certainly tipped a little bit. We must try it again some time, we said, when the opportunity arose.

It arose one night at Mr Chidley's. As you may remember, he played cards at Mrs Charleycott's every night. His boots clattered through the stone-flagged passage past our sitting-room door on his way out at exactly five to seven, and at exactly twenty-five to eleven they clattered back. When Charles was on duty at the camp in the evenings and I was alone in the house, I read or sewed or wrote letters. When he wasn't on duty, we read, he painted, or sometimes we had friends in. One pair of friends in particular: Charles's colleague Andrew Thornton and his wife Jane, who shared so many of our interests. Walking, painting, books ... We tried our hands at clay modelling, too, and were particularly keen on it at the time.

It was fun to model as a foursome and compare results, but there were snags about doing it at their place. They lodged with a maiden lady whose former front parlour was their sitting-room and the table had a red plush cloth with bobbles on it. There was a matching drape with bobbles round the mantelpiece, too, and a Brussels carpet and a piano with filigree brass candlesticks. The carpet was ancient and the piano wouldn't play on account of the damp in the hammers, but nevertheless the room had the air of a Buckingham Palace stateroom about it: a sort of hallowed atmosphere; of infinite preservation. One couldn't slap clay about in those surroundings.

Not even in secret, hoping to clear up afterwards. Miss Rice lived in the back room, the Thorntons in the front, and there was no separate hallway leading to the street. When she went out she had to pass through their room, and she seemed to go through on a revolving band. We had supper there once. She went through at least six times — and six times back again — her eyes whizzing about behind her glasses like pinballs, looking us over, seeing what we were eating, making sure her possessions were intact. One speck of clay on her red plush tablecloth and the Thorntons would be out on their ear.

We couldn't do our modelling at Miss Rice's so we did it instead at Mr Chidley's, where I could mop the clay off the lino next morning. Where we could put newspapers on the table and if the surface got smeared I could polish that next morning, too. Where we had the place to ourselves, Mr Chidley being along at Mrs Charleycott's, and we could talk and model in freedom until it reached the witching hour of twenty-five to eleven, when Mr Chidley came through the front door.

Clatter went his boots through to the kitchen, clatter on out to the yard — Mr Chidley had gone to the earth-closet. Clatter back in again, through the parlour, up the stairs, the sound of boots being discarded. A creak of bedsprings — Mr Chidley slept right over our sitting-room — and then the silence of somebody waiting.

What Mr Chidley was waiting for was for the Thorntons to go home. He always knew when they were there. If they hadn't gone by eleven, the boots began to be picked up and dropped like the fall of an auctioneer's hammer. As soon as the Thorntons went, the thudding stopped. By the time we went upstairs ourselves Mr Chidley would be snoring with the mighty roll of a September tide on the Cornish cliffs, having settled matters to his satisfaction. He wouldn't have snored so soundly the night we did the table-turning, though, if he'd known what had happened to his horsehair chair.

This happened very innocently, too. We'd invited the Thorntons round and worked on our models for a while. Charles and Andrew were doing heads, I remember, Jane was working on a stylised hedgehog and I was doing a horse. We stopped for coffee and sandwiches, chatted about this and that, and somehow the conversation turned to off-beat matters. The business of somebody sitting on a chair, for instance, and two people each putting a hand on the top of his head for a while and the other hand under his armpits; then whipping the hands off his head, lifting simultaneously with the others, when even a twelve-stone subject should waft up like a feather. We tried it with Jane but couldn't make it work. It was something to do with the pressure. She should have gone right up to the ceiling, said Andrew. He'd definitely read about it happening.

This reminded Charles of his father's account of the table going through the window. Had they ever done any table-turning? he asked. All we needed was a small round table. Now where had he seen the very thing? I knew but I wasn't saying. It didn't take Charles long to remember, though. It was under Mr Chidley's aspidistra in the passage.

Within no time Charles and Andrew were shifting the heavy pot. It took the pair of them with bended knees to lift it. Why didn't they try the hands-on hands-off system on that? I asked. Charles said we were supposed to be being *serious*. I was. I told them not to put the pot on the horsehair chair that stood rigidly by the side of the table. Nonsense,

said Charles. That wouldn't harm the chair. It would be quicker, too, if they had to nip the pot back in a hurry, supposing old man Chidley came back early.

That was all I needed. That table wouldn't turn. Andrew and Jane were frankly sceptical. As for me, my mind was on Mr Chidley coming through the front door and seeing where we'd put his aspidistra, and I couldn't have contacted any spirits if they'd been there. Charles, determined not to be beaten, kept saying we must try again, consequently it must have been a good twenty-five past ten when the aspidistra was re-ensconced on the table, leaving a circular indentation on the horsehair chair-seat that looked as if somebody had been at it with a bucket-sized pie-cutter.

'That'll come out,' Charles said airily. 'All it needs is for somebody to sit on it for a while.' Me of course, as I was the only one who appeared to be the least bit worried about it. I sat on it till I heard Mr Chidley's footsteps on the pavement outside, when I fled into the sitting-room to join the others. I sat on it frantically later, while Charles was seeing the Thorntons off at the front door, the three of them laughing at some joke like demented drains while boots rattled like mad upstairs. I was up at five next morning, sitting on it in the dark, trying to iron the indentation out. It was no use. By the time I left to catch the bus to town the circle was still as visible as ever.

I worried. It was Friday. The day when Mrs Charleycott came to do the cleaning. *She'd* spot the damage, if he didn't. I crept guiltily into the house that night — I always got in ahead of Charles — expecting the balloon to go up in earnest. A row at least. Maybe he'd give us notice, and where, in that village, would we get other digs? Not only was the place packed with people living out from camp, but what sort of reference would Mr Chidley give us? That we'd ruined his chairs? Poked holes through his saucepan? (That had happened the previous week.) I couldn't be sure that he didn't know about the lino or the towel-stand, either. I was away all day and, human nature being what it is, he might have looked round in our absence.

Nothing happened. Whether Mrs Charleycott had been in a hurry that day and had merely flicked a duster over the chair ... Whether, if she had seen it, she'd put it down to Mrs Thompson ... One can't notice everything exactly on the dot, and Mrs T. did have a reputation.

No. What Mr Chidley was most concerned with when I got indoors was that the front door lock was broken. The tumblers had gone. You couldn't open it with the key, he said: 'twould have to be took off and properly mended. Must have been us lettin' them friends of ours out. It had been all right before.

It hadn't. It had been like the lock on Enna's mother's earth-closet. You had to fiddle the key around to make it work. If the tumblers had finally got fed up and fallen out, it certainly wasn't before time. However, I happily said we'd pay for it. It was worth it if that was the reason he hadn't noticed the dent in the chair-seat, which faded, I'm glad to say, within a week.

Mr Chidley's possessions did seem fated, though. I wondered what would disintegrate next.

Chapter Eight

Living at Mr Chidley's wasn't at all like being in Emma's village. There Louisa and I, as Enna's friends and frequent visitors, had been accepted as if we were relations: invited into people's houses, recognised in the village shop, included in the lych-gate gossip after church. In wartime, in Mr Chidley's village, things were different. We were outsiders: people who came and went at the drop of a posting list. The inhabitants might be willing to let living-out quarters to naval personnel—they'd never made money so easily in their lives—but that itself marked the newcomers as outsiders. People who'd pay thirty shillings for a couple of rooms when the rent of the whole cottage was only ten! 'Got their wallets where their brains is' was the way the villagers put it, and they treated us as a race apart accordingly.

That didn't stop them being inquisitive about what we did, however—in our case particularly Mrs Charleycott, who, having a grown-up son at home and so not having room for lodgers herself, overcame this drawback by taking an interest in whoever was at Mr Chidley's. Thus it was that when I poked the holes through the old boy's saucepan, I traced a replica a good week later, after considerable searching in town, with the idea of

simply replacing it and saying nothing, which would save a lot of explanation. It was just as well that I changed my mind and confessed when I got it home, because it so happened that Mrs Charleycott had been in the store as well, had seen me buying the saucepan and, recognising the pattern as the one favoured by the menage Chidley (brown enamel with a flat tin lid and a painted wooden knob on top) had — returning to the village on the four o'clock bus whereas I didn't get home till five — beaten an immediate path to Mr Chidley's and told him what she'd seen.

What I'd wanted to conceal from him wasn't so much that I'd ruined his saucepan as that I'd done it by making mintoes in it. I'd never have lived it down. Life was real and life was earnest in the country, and one didn't waste time and money on making sweets. The thing was, though, I'd come across this recipe and my mouth had watered at the thought of it, sweets being rationed to twelve ounces per person per month. I'd best not give the exact proportions or there may be more ruined saucepans about, but it involved boiling margarine, sugar and golden syrup together for several minutes, stirring in eight heaped tablespoonfuls of powdered milk, adding peppermint essence, stirring again over the heat till thick — and then immediately, on account of it setting very quickly, scooping the mixture out in teaspoonfuls and rolling it rapidly between one's hands into balls.

Where I fell down was over the rolling. Unless you had

asbestos hands you couldn't possibly do it rapidly: it was like juggling with liquid lava. Consequently by the time I had six successful mintoes cooling on a plate, the rest of the mixture had set like concrete and nothing I could do would get it out.

I have read somewhere since that they make white piano keys from powdered milk. Quite likely from this very recipe. It certainly set hard enough in the pan. I attacked it with the carving fork, which I hit using the poker as a hammer. That simply bent the fork. I tried to loosen it round the sides with one of Mr Chidley's ancient pointed dinner knives. All that happened was that the point came off. Eventually I succeeded in getting the stuff out by using a tablespoon as a battering ram, but it was more than a Chidley saucepan could stand. When I held it up to the light it was like looking at a galaxy of stars, there were so many holes in the bottom. My only consolation was that I'd been making the mintoes on our sitting-room fire with the door shut, having had an idea that Mr Chidley wouldn't approve. He therefore didn't know about it, and if I could get an identical replacement — *if* I could in wartime — this was one of my lapses about which he need never know.

We had separate sets of saucepans on separate shelves and he hadn't noticed that one of mine was missing, so when I found the replacement I could hardly believe my luck. Except, as I realised the more I looked at it, the new saucepan was shinier and heavier. His looked worn and thin. Even if I substituted the old cover he'd be bound to spot the different pan underneath by comparison. There was nothing for it but to confess to him after all. So I marched boldly out to the kitchen with it, wrapped, saying 'Here's a present for you, Mr Chidley. I bet you can't guess what it is,' and he, regarding me from his armchair with an expression like that of Judge Jeffreys — who operated around those parts after the Monmouth Rebellion and no doubt had an assistant called Charleycott — said, 'Ah I can. A new saucepan theest bought at Whites. What happened to the old 'un?'

Explanations followed. I managed to avoid the express mention of mintoes by saying I'd boiled dried milk in it and ruined the bottom when I tried to clean it. 'Why din't 'ee let I have 'n? I could have got he clean,' he said. 'What have 'ee done with 'n?' he went on to ask, another thought crossing his mind. 'Put it in the Food Office dustbin,' I told him. 'There wasn't any point in bringing it back.' Mr Chidley regarded me disapprovingly. 'I could have mended he with pot-repairers,' he said.

Which, of course, was why I hadn't brought it back. I was getting wise to his make-do and mending. It would have been studded with them like limpet mines — round metal pot-menders, impossible to clean properly, harbouring germs — and I'd have had to go on using it, while the new one sat in splendour on Mr Chidley's shelf, no doubt being saved for his grandchildren.

So I'd got myself a new saucepan and had my first experience of rural M.I.5, after which I kept a weather eye open for Mrs Charleycott. I knew the days she went to town and often, in my lunchtime, I would nip smartly up a side street or into a shop when I spotted a familiar royal-blue-coated figure in the offing. Not that I was up to anything nefarious. I wasn't ruining Mr Chidley's property all the time. But she always looked as if she thought I was, and I dodged automatically when I saw her.

I had no chance of dodging the day she caught me with the gypsies, though. I was outnumbered by ten to one.

It had never occurred to me, until I went to work in the Food Office, that the war could have an effect on people like gypsies, who normally live their lives as far removed from authority and its complexities as possible. But they had to eat. They needed ration cards for tea and sugar and bread, for instance, even if, with rabbits and pheasants falling fortuitously into their cook-pots at every turn, they weren't so concerned about meat as the rest of us with our meagre one-and-twopence worth per week. Clothing coupons, too, were as good as a handout of money. Fancy authority giving them something they could sell! You could get five pounds on the black market for a book of them — and whoever heard of a gypsy buying new clothes?

Initially they'd had to be issued with identity cards, of course. I don't know how that had been managed, national registration having taken place in 1938. Probably registration officers went to the various camps and drove themselves dotty trying to sort out birth dates and family names. But there they were, registered, and anything deriving from the fact — like having to renew ration books or get temporary ration cards when they moved about (down-country for the pea-picking, or up to Evesham in August for the plums) — brought them into the Food Office like a swarm of bees and presented just about as many problems.

For one thing, en masse, they smelled. Outdoors it wasn't so noticeable, but in the confines of the Food Office in warm or wet weather the effect of peat-smoke and unwashedness was overpowering. We opened the windows, surreptitiously, so as not to hurt their feelings: when one knew them they were charming people. We dealt with them out of turn, in the hope of getting them back out into the open quickly — somehow it never worked. They *liked* coming to the Food Office. It was a social occasion for them. Only the women came, never the men. They combined getting ration cards, or expectant mothers' orange juice, or registering the resultant babies when they arrived, with trips to town to sell clothes pegs or paper flowers and invariably trooped in looking like the chorus from *Carmen*: cigarettes in their mouths, babies wrapped in shawls in their arms, large gypsy baskets on their hips.

While we dealt with the principal customer — usually an expectant mother, who would be accompanied to the counter by her mother or special friends — the rest of the band ranged themselves happily round the room on the wooden waiting chairs and proceeded to make themselves at home. They brought shop-bought sponge cakes from their baskets and passed them round from hand to hand, taking communal bites till they were gone. They produced bottles of pop which they shared in the same way, up-ending the bottles appreciatively. They were reported to have been seen, in the cul-de-sac round the corner from the Food Office, doing the same with the official issue of concentrated orange juice, the mother-to-be standing by with a 'have-this-one-on-me-girls' air while the rest of the band drank it neat from the bottle.

It probably didn't matter very much. She in turn would share someone else's bottle. Nearly all the younger women were pregnant. There was a gloriously accommodating attitude to that condition, too, which sometimes led to difficulties.

Some gypsies, I was told by the senior clerk, Miss Blick, were married properly under true gypsy law: others 'jumped the sticks, then lived together. Others again — the rebels who occur in every walk of life — merely dallied when they felt like it in the moon daisies. Since gypsy women didn't take their husband's name when they married, this could be somewhat confusing. I stood by one day while Miss Blick explained to a black-eyed beauty who would have knocked them flat had she ever got to Hollywood — I could see her barefoot and blown-skirted on a cliff-top, the Corsair's woman, with Errol Flynn bounding about on the rocks at the bottom — that with an infant fifteen months old and another on the way, she was probably entitled to free milk and vitamins.

'How much does your husband allow you?' Miss Blick enquired, preparing to fill in the forms. The raven-haired ravisher assumed a soulful expression 'Aint got no husband, Mum, worse luck,' she said. 'Only what I earns meself and the bit me poor old mother gives me.'

She got her free milk and vitamins and in due course the baby arrived and was brought into the Food Office by the mother and supporting band. Beautifully dressed in a spotless robe, they were as proud of him as if he were a prince. Admittedly it was with an eye to business — it had already become an established gypsy custom to bring in the newborn baby and show him, so that the staff could cross his palm with silver — but there was a friendliness about it too, an atmosphere of timid trust. Here there were people who didn't shoo them off or threaten to call the police, who genuinely seemed to like them. Miss Blick, who mostly dealt with them, became their confidante and advised them on many matters.

On the days they came to town she would often be late back from lunch, having met up with them in the street. I saw her several times myself, surrounded by a laughing colourful group, while passers-by looked on in astonishment. Usually gypsies go by as a remotely separate unit, save for the offer of bunches of primroses or heather. I felt quite envious, thinking how satisfying it must be to be accepted by the wild ones like that.

My turn was to come, however, after I'd served my apprenticeship. Came the day when they hailed me, too, in the street, gathering round me with their baskets as they had Miss Blick, offering me a sticky iced bun. At which moment in time—an expression I normally dislike but that moment was certainly time-stopping—I spotted an outsize royal-blue coat on the other side of the street and Mrs Charleycott's incredulous face above it.

Mr Chidley was waiting for me when I got home. 'Theest want to be careful,' he warned me. 'Start hob-nobbing with diddecois and theest find theeself murdered in thee bed.' Hardly, with him and Charles in the house, and anyway the gypsies weren't like that. I explained about knowing them through the Food Office. That only made it worse. Working for officialdom and in so doing getting acquainted with gypsies, I was out on both sides of the count. Not so much with Mr Chidley, who treated Charles and me generally as if he'd adopted us, and me personally as a particularly misguided granddaughter, but by the time Mrs Charleycott had passed on the tale, I got some pretty odd looks around the village.

I was regarded with suspicion in the village shop in any case, presumably as a Food Office spy. I never came in for any of the little bonuses with which shopkeepers occasionally rewarded their registered customers: when, for example, they managed to get a crate of oranges, or an extra case of eggs from somewhere.

We were at the Thorntons one night when Jane announced that she'd been given three eggs that day at Weston's. In wartime that was like three dozen. I was round at the shop at half-past eight next morning, duly armed with my ration book. Mr Weston collected together my meagre weekly supply of groceries. Not a single egg emerged from under the counter. I would have asked about them earlier but waited until the order was completed in case he brought them out as a surprise at the end. I was just about to say I'd heard there'd been a handout when somebody prodded me matily in the back. It was Jane. If I mentioned it now he'd know who told me and she'd be in the soup. Extra eggs were non-existent so far as I was concerned. It was as bad as being a policeman.

One day, by mistake, he gave me extra cheese — somebody else's ration. I didn't realise it until I got home and discovered the two little greaseproof packets. They were absolutely minuscule — we got two ounces each a week — but one packet was slightly larger than the other. Obviously a three-ration family: six ounces instead of four. I took it back immediately. Mr Weston didn't thank me. Just took it and weighed it to see I'd brought back the bigger portion. Would he have done that with one of the regular villagers? I wondered. Or did he think I was setting a Food Office trap?

The village butcher was quite different. A giant of a man with black curly hair, who looked as if he ought to have been the village blacksmith, he ran his business from what at first glance appeared to be an ordinary house in a row in the High Street. You went through the front door and turned into a dim-lit, stone-floored room containing a chopping-block and a carcase on a hook. A tray of sausages stood on a side-table, another of home-made faggots beside it. That was the set-up, take it or leave it, where Henry Barnes ruled supreme. When a bullock's carcase hung from the hook, everybody who came in had beef. When that was gone, he brought in a pig and the next lot of customers had pork. No nonsense about what you thought you'd like. You took what you were given. First-class meat it invariably was, too, and not too much bothering about the ration. *He* didn't seem worried by my Food Office connection. Maybe he didn't know about it. Or was there perhaps some slight reference to it when, parcelling me up a couple of pre-war-sized pork chops, he would say, 'Can't expect me to cut 'em to the pennyworth, now, can they? Be more waste than 'twould be worth.'

A butcher's shop like that wouldn't be permitted nowadays. It wouldn't be considered hygienic. For a start, the reason he dealt with only one carcase at a time was that he had no refrigeration—just a stone-floored, stone-walled room, naturally cold because of its construction. He was a professional in his trade, though: the meat he sold was perfect and he seemed to have more of it at his disposal than anyone in town. No one questioned where it came from. Maybe it was all above board. He was just fairer with us, and countenanced no under-the-counter business in his apportioning. Nobody would have dared to question his decision anyway. Henry Barnes was a giant of a man.

He had his Achilles heel, though. Charles and I explored the countryside enthusiastically in Charles's off-duty periods. We were always coming back and telling Mr Chidley where we'd been, and he would tell us the history of wherever it was, with a colloquial tale or two thrown in.

Up round by the mill? That went back a bit. Supposed to be in the Domesday Book. Water-lilies was a sight worth seeing there in summer, too. A fair place for courtin' couples. 'Seed Mrs Charleycott up there once,' he reminisced. 'That was when she was Bessie Winters. Never think it to look at her now... I always thought she'd have married old Stan.' The late Mr Charleycott's name had been Bert. Who, I wondered, was Stan? I tried to imagine her as a young girl, on the grassy bank amid the sorrel and the buttercups, the mill-wheel creaking lazily, the pond a sheet of huge pink water-lilies, blue dragonflies flitting gauzily above them. A young lad gazing ardently down into Mrs Charleycott's eyes: Mrs Charleycott gazing ardently back.

Alas, I could see her only as a fat woman in a bright blue coat, with short straight hair and a disapproving expression. So swiftly went the transient years. Poor Mrs Charleycott. It happened eventually to all of us.

Another day we found our way to a village called Limington where, four hundred years before Mrs Charleycott's dalliance by the millpond, another youthful spirit had had its carefree fling. A curate named Thomas Wolsey, who'd been put in the stocks for getting scandalously drunk at the Lopen feast. He later became Cardinal Wolsey, prelate of all England. Mr Chidley had never heard of him. All he wanted to know, when we said we'd been to Limington, was had we seen anything odd when we'd passed a certain field gate, a little way out from our own village along the Limington road.

No, we said, we hadn't. Mr Chidley informed us that it was haunted. By a girl in a bonnet and old-fashioned dress, he said. People'd see her beckoning from the field, twenty yards or so inside the gate, then she'd turn, looking back as if she wanted them to follow her. Whatever it was she wanted to lead them to — gold coins some said, but maybe 'twas her own remains, though nobody'd ever heard of a murder done thereabouts — one or two had gone after her but they'd never found a thing. She always kept ahead of them and vanished into the clump of trees in the furthest corner.

Had he seen her himself? I asked. No, said Mr Chidley. But Harry Barnes and his missus Milly had, back when they were courting. 'Did *he* go after her?' I enquired, visualising the brawny figure of the butcher climbing the gate and striding determinedly across the field. 'Did *he* see anything before she disappeared?'

'Din' get that far,' said Mr Chidley happily. 'Accordin' to Milly, the minute he seed her he fainted.'

Chapter Nine

After that, if Charles had had his way, we'd have gone via the haunted gate on every walk. As it was, when we did, he always lingered, peering hopefully over it for the ghost, while I went past it with my eyes shut. Once we did the Limington walk twice in one day. It was strawberry time I remember and Mr Chidley had told us that they grew wild in Ashington woods, with fruit the size of blackberries.

They did. We should have taken basins. Stupidly we took paper bags, plastic ones not yet having been invented. I can see us now in a clearing that could have been the setting for Botticelli's *Primavera*. The grass a brilliant emerald, studded with buttercups and daisies and the delicate pink-mauve spikes of lady's smock. Birds singing in the trees behind us. A cuckoo, the eternally magic symbol of an English summer, calling hauntingly, elusively, in the distance. The sun pouring down. Two brown paper bags filled with strawberries on the grass beside us — I was intending to make them into jam. And Charles, looking as out of place in naval uniform in such a setting as if he'd walked on in it in *A Midsummer Night's Dream* — but in wartime wearing it everywhere was compulsory — trying not to get it too dirty as, with his fingers, he removed a thorn from the paw of an enormous dog.

It had tacked on to us as we went through Limington, limping even then, but nothing we could do would turn it back. We shooed it, ignored it, stopped at a gate pretending that was as far as we were going: the dog sat down behind us and waited. We almost gave up the idea of going on to Ashington, it was hobbling so pitifully behind us, but what could we have done if we hadn't? We didn't know where it belonged and we hesitated attempting to look at its collar. It appeared to be a cross between a collie and a St Bernard, the collie being the biting end. It showed the whites of its eyes when we spoke to it, even while the St Bernard end wagged its tail.

So it followed us to Ashington woods and lay down while we picked the strawberries, using the time to bite at its foot. 'It's not his leg that's hurt,' said Charles. 'He's got something in his paw. Come on, boy, let me have a look.' And I'm darned if that dog didn't. His eyes, pure St Bernard now, turned up in lugubrious self-pity, while Charles pulled out a blackberry thorn and I, kneeling anxiously by, waited for a snarling attack at any moment.

It didn't happen. Charles got the thorn out. The dog bounced about, barking in appreciation. Charles chanced his arm and grabbed its collar. Charles's arm was safe from that dog till the end of time — all it did was lick his face —

but there wasn't an address on the collar. When we started back for Mr Chidley's the dog accompanied us, jumping affectionately up at us as we walked. Splosh went my bag of strawberries down my pale green sprigged summer dress. Splosh went Charles's down his uniform. Plonk went paws the size of a bear's feet, grinding in the strawberry juice, alternately, all the way back to Mr Chidley's.

We'd thought the dog would leave us in Limington, where he'd picked us up, or that after that he'd soon turn back. He didn't, and any gesture we made to shoo him off only made him leap joyfully up all the more. My dress didn't look very green-sprigged now. Mrs Charleycott would have thought I'd joined the gypsies.

At Mr Chidley's we turned round again. We couldn't just abandon the dog outside the door. In any case, Charles had to go on duty that evening. Supposing it followed him up to the camp? Charles might have got away with wearing shirts with orange stripes, but he'd never get away with cycling up complete with an attendant dog the size of a Shetland pony. We couldn't take him into the house with us, either. One sweep of his tail and Mr Chidley would be sticking up everything in sight for weeks. It was back to Limington where, even if it wasn't his home, somebody might recognise him and know where he belonged.

Up the road once more, past the haunted gate. Tired as I was, I closed my eyes automatically. Past it three times in one day — it wasn't half tempting fate, and I bet that blasted dog wouldn't have done a thing to protect us. In Limington we almost wondered if the dog had been a ghost itself, it disappeared so fast. One moment it was padding behind us. The next minute it had gone. There wasn't a soul in sight whom we could ask. Three hours following us as if it was glued to us, though, and then vanishing so suddenly, in a flash?

It had gone, anyway. We went ourselves while the going was good. Down the road past the haunted gate for the fourth time. I was too tired now, though, to close my eyes, and even Charles didn't linger to look over it. After all of which, when we told Mr Chidley, he said, 'Cor, fancy takin' *he* back. He do know his way around better than anybody.'

The dog, it transpired, belonged at one of the farms and did a farm-dog's work in the mornings. In the afternoons, though, when he wasn't wanted for anything, it was his habit to lie by the side of the road and tack on to passing walkers. He'd go with them for company, leaving them when they came back through Limington or, if they didn't, cutting across the fields when it was time for the evening milking. It must have been the special circumstances of Charles getting the thorn out that made him follow us right back to Mr Chidley's. Equally it must have been milking time when we finally returned with him to Limington and he'd shot off to fetch the cows.

'Gosh,' I said, 'we were beginning to wonder whether he was a ghost.' Mr Chidley laughed his head off at the thought. When I said we'd passed the haunted gate four times, though, and hadn't seen a thing, he said, 'Thee wust lucky, wussn't?' Where, I wondered, was the difference? Couldn't a dog be a ghost as well?

After that we stopped doing the Limington walk in case the dog followed us again. In view of the haunted gate I wasn't sorry. There were other walks and excursions, though, that I remember to this day, fresh as I then was to the country. Along the river where a kingfisher hunted, for instance. The only kingfisher I have ever seen at such close quarters. I can see even now the electric blue flash of his wings as he hurtled upstream against the background of bulrushes.

Across the marshes beyond the river was a tree where a barn owl lived. We used to watch him at dusk when Charles's duty turns permitted, hunting low along the hedgerows with his three-foot wingspan like a restless, arm-waving spirit. I wasn't afraid of him, though. In imagination I flew with him. One night Charles had to go on duty and, having stayed near the owl-tree longer than we intended, we took a short cut across the fields. One of Charles's inspired short cuts which so often, to his surprise, brought us out somewhere completely different from where we'd intended.

In this case we emerged two miles up the main road. Whether Charles would be late for duty was my principal worry. His, according to my diary, was first of all whether any of his colleagues seeing us would think we were walking the five miles out from town to save the bus fare (what else, he said despairingly, *would* anyone be doing walking along a dead straight, uninteresting road at dusk on a summer's evening?): and secondly, when I started to hiccup as a result of worrying and hurrying at the same time, whether whoever saw us would also think I was drunk.

All was well. Nobody saw us, and he reported for duty on time. But we weren't so fortunate on another excursion — this time on our bikes, one Saturday afternoon — to a village where there was a particularly ancient market cross. The question was, it being dull and overcast, was it going to rain? Charles didn't want to get his uniform wet. It would be uncomfortable, it wouldn't do the uniform much good, and once again it was his duty night. We consulted Mr Chidley who, after due deliberation, announced that it was going to be fine 'cos stones was heavin'.

This, interpreted, meant that the flagstones in the passage were sweating. They often did in hot weather. We took him at his word and went. Twelve miles, mostly pushing uphill, to a village where there was indeed a market cross — we managed to get a glimpse of the top of it — but surrounded as it was by U.S. army jeeps, gum-chewing G.Is. and their attendant flock of British Betty Grables, somehow it had lost its significance. It looked like a downtrodden, shabby old relic in the middle of a maypole dance. We were thankful that the Americans *had* come over — we could never have won the war without them — but they did somehow leave their mark upon a place and make us realise how behind the times we were.

It started to rain. We took refuge in Ye Olde Market Crosse Tearooms. The G.Is. were there in force as well, crowded into the high-backed inglenook benches, gazing in disbelief at our watered-down wartime brew, wondering, from their expressions, what all the fuss in Boston Harbour had been about.

They weren't all as they have so often been painted. Inevitably some had already acquired girlfriends and were dazzling them with tales of the high life back in the good old U.S., but at the next table to ours two somewhat older soldiers sat huddled over a sheaf of photographs. 'Eighteen months old,' one of them said. 'When I get back home he won't even know me. When I unlatch the gate he'll say to my wife, "Momma, who dat strange man coming up the path?"'

He laughed, but there was longing in his voice. I stole a look across. He was holding a photograph of a girl with a baby in her arms — looking at it but obviously not seeing it. In imagination he was three thousand miles away, walking up a New England path.

A short while before, that had been Charles and Simmy, gazing up at the moon over the desert. Two-and-a-half years we'd been apart. It could happen again at any moment. It was a reminder to make the most of the present — which was why, when we came out of the tearooms to find that it was pouring (thundering and lightning, too, by this time), I donned my cycling cape lightheartedly. Who cared about it raining? It could snow if it liked, so long as Charles and I were together.

Charles, who didn't have a cape, wasn't feeling quite so romantic. He could see himself getting very wet. And it was impossible for us to shelter: he had to be on duty at seven. There was nothing we could do but ride for it. If he rode behind me, I, in my cape, might give him some protection I suggested. So, Charles breathing vengeance on Mr Chidley and his weather forecasts, we cycled home. Fortunately mostly downhill, except that the rain was in our faces and, intensified by our downhill swoop, it was as if we'd had a hose turned on us. It ran down my neck, and I got wet in spite of my cape. Charles, behind, was soaked. Halfway home he defied regulations and stuffed his cap inside his coat

— he only had one cap, he said, and it felt already as if it had shrunk. It hadn't, though he had to wear it damp for days and got a cold as a result. He had a spare uniform though, and changing rapidly and putting on his oilskins, once more made it to the camp on time.

He even had time to talk to Mr Chidley, who came clattering out from his kitchen as soon as he heard us push our bikes in. 'How far've 'ee bin?' enquired Mr Chidley cheerfully. And in the same breath, 'Did 'ee get wet?' We did, said Charles, the water dripping from him as he stood in the passage, as from a saturated Old English sheepdog. *What* was it Mr Chidley had said about the flagstones heaving? Ah, said Mr Chidley... They heaved either for heat, or for rain when 'twas a thunderstorm comin', and, by golly, hadn't we had a big 'un?

So we snatched such pleasure as we could against a background of England at war. The Allies had now landed in Europe. Convoys of tanks rolled through the village day and night, rumbling down to the coast. Charles and his colleagues worked all hours up at the camp. Any day now they expected to be posted. Rumour had it that they were destined for Japanese waters as soon as the fighting in Europe ended.

Behind all this, like the background of a tapestry, the life of the village continued. War or not, the tank convoys halted when the cows plodded up the road to the various farms at milking time, or a haycart creaked and swayed along ahead of them. A woman on a bicycle, in a brown felt

hat and a milking coat, brought milk round the village in two large cans on her handlebars. Definitely a mark of progress, that. Once she'd have carried them suspended from a wooden yoke on her shoulders. She ladled the milk into jugs which people put on the pavement outside their front doors, protected from dust by saucers. The milk wasn't pasteurised; it was straight from the cow and usually still warm when we got it. Fourpence a pint — two new pence, that is — and there was no milk rationing in the country.

For coolness we kept our jug alongside Mr Chidley's, on the stone platform in the former beer room — at least we did till I went in there one day and saw Mr Chidley's cat with its head in his jug (ours was covered with a muslin cloth weighted with coloured beads, thoughtfully sent down by my grandmother.) When I told Mr Chidley, he said, 'Thass all right. I don't drink it cold, I puts it in me tea.' After which enlightenment on rural attitudes to hygiene, I kept ours inside the meatsafe. Muslin covers could be pawed off by cats — and put back again by their not-too-particular owners.

After a while my shelf in the safe began to look rather crowded, the milk-jug having been joined by the frying-pan. There were two, if you remember, Mr Chidley's and ours, hanging side by side on the wall. Mr Chidley had told us what a good mouser Spotso was, and one day he must have chased a mouse up the wall and, seeking for refuge in a place that looked like Colditz, the poor little thing must have dived down the nearest hollow frying-pan handle with such force that it got stuck. *Our* frying-pan handle, of course. I didn't use it very often, what with the bacon and cooking fat ration being minimal and wartime

sausages being less than exciting. In consequence, when I did take it down, the mouse had been dead for quite some time and its tail was sticking out of the frying-pan handle stiff as a board. I screeched and dropped the pan. Mr Chidley came running, Charles not being back yet from the camp. ''Tis only a mouse,' said Mr Chidley tapping it out. 'A liddle thing like that won't hurt 'ee.'

Maybe not, particularly since it was dead, but I didn't fancy the frying-pan again. So I bought a new one, and kept it in the meat-safe. Mr Chidley said I wun't half fussy . . . I can't say I was surprised when, a week or two later, Mrs Charleycott went down with stomach trouble. Not that I'm suggesting she had dead mice down *her* frying-pan handle, but country people certainly did seem to ask for it.

Mrs Charleycott was a large fat woman and inclined to have a wheezy chest. A couple of days in bed with stomach trouble and Mrs Charleycott developed bronchitis. Another day or two — it was a very wet summer and there was always a mist in the mornings over the moors — and Mrs Charleycott had pneumonia. It was all so sudden. One day there she was sailing conspicuously up the High Street in town — even in summer she wore her royal blue coat: no wonder, according to Charles, who reckoned that with her waist measurement anything she wore had to be constructed by a tent-maker — eyes swivelling around like submarine periscopes, looking for me, while I nipped smartly up a side street . . . And only a week later there she was, not expected to live, her tent-coat hanging silent in the wardrobe, while I, filled with remorse, as people inevitably are in such circumstances, wished I hadn't been so mean to her. Though as Charles pointed out, if I *had* stopped and let her see that I'd been buying kippers, it would hardly have prevented her pneumonia.

Mr Chidley gave us regular bulletins. The doctor had visited her three times in one day. Her temperature was over a hundred and four. Her breathing was getting worse. One night I opened our door as I heard him going past on his way to bed. 'How is Mrs C. today?' I asked. He said nothing. Just shook his head.

I lay awake for hours that night, pondering the inexorableness of existence. People worked hard, had their modest pleasures, knew sadness, grew old; found companionship in their old age, as had Mrs Charleycott and Mr Chidley. In the end though, while the backcloth of the pageant might seem unchanging, one by one the players departed from the scene. It was happening now with Mrs Charleycott. How would Mr Chidley take it?

There were no roof-lifting snores from the next room that night. Mr Chidley, too, lay awake. Eventually I must have dozed off, though. I woke to hear, through our open window, a horse whinnying close at hand and, or was I imagining it, there was an answering whinny in the distance, and the faint sound of hoofbeats on the road.

Charles was awake too. We were out of bed and at the window in an instant. It was bright moonlight, and, looking across into the farmyard opposite, we could see the farmer's shire mare Bess, whom he used for ploughing, rearing excitedly on the end of a long rope. Even while we wondered why she was tethered, and why the farmer didn't come out at her whinnying, the distant hoofbeats grew nearer—and down the road, right in the middle, came clattering another enormous shire-horse, the absolute image of Bess. Beneath our window it turned, gathered itself, and jumped the five-barred gate into the farmyard. Now we realised what was happening. This was a stallion and he was answering Bess.

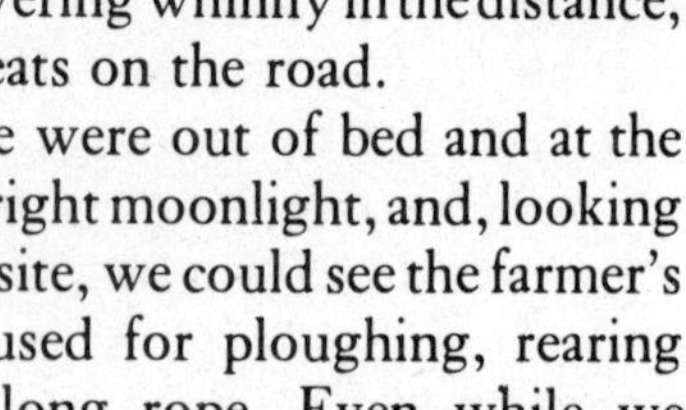

The two horses met. Both palest dapple-grey with huge fringed feet and silver manes, they looked like lengendary knightly chargers in the moonlight. We watched from the window entranced. Even as we debated whether we ought to tell the farmer, there was a rattle of bolts across the way and a torchlight appeared in the yard. Satisfied that matters were in hand we went back to bed. Suddenly I felt more tranquil. This was the pattern of village life — of all life. Mrs Charleycott going. The horses mating.

A clever bit of husbandry that. We pieced it together next day. Bess in season. The farmer tethering her in the yard, out of her stable, knowing that there was a champion shire stallion at a farm outside the village, who, as stallions do, had jumped his home hedge and come galloping to do his stuff. At no charge to Bess's owner, of course. It wasn't *his* fault that the stallion got out.

What was more, Mrs Charleycott recovered. That was the night her temperature went down. Within another week — it was that sort of pneumonia, apparently — Mr Chidley was up at her house playing cards. In no time at all, it seemed, there she was again, burgeoning down the High Street in town, looking for all the world like a blue-spinnakered boat in full sail, while I dodged her up a side-turning. I was jolly glad to see her back — but so much for my good intentions!

Chapter Ten

Meantime our rented chattels went on falling apart, and when I reported the damage to Mr Chidley he continued, though she had now been gone for months, to attribute the blame to Mrs Thompson. Whether she had indeed been exceptionally heavy-handed and he really believed it was her fault, or whether he was being tactful — blaming the previous tenant and my turn would come when in due course I had a successor — the fact remained that she took the rap in absentia for some pretty remarkable happenings.

When the blades of the dinner-knives started to snap off — for instance, if you remember, I broke one hacking at the mintoe mixture — I didn't mention it to Mr Chidley until a second one went a few weeks later. The truth of the matter was that they were made of old-fashioned steel, worn thin by years of use and cleaning. The blades were down to stiletto points and the points were so thin they curled, but when I presented them to Mr Chidley he said at once, 'That were Mrs Thompson. She were always opening tins with 'em.'

How he knew — and how she could have opened a tin with a knife that bent the moment you tried to cut an egg with it — something I have puzzled over many times since. Tactfully I said nothing, however, just accepted the stainless ones he gave me. Normally these were kept in their cardboard box in his sideboard and we were permitted to borrow them if we had guests. I did hope we might have won them for good now: it would have been one small item of modern advancement. But no. By next day he'd re-rounded the tops of the old knives and the new ones went back into the sideboard to be kept for best.

The same thing happened when the armchair went through the floor one night when Charles and I were sitting in it together. A common enough habit with young marrieds, sharing the same armchair, but it doesn't usually subside beneath them like the sinking of the *Titanic*. Actually the fault lay in the chair legs — sharp little pointed Victorian ones, with lethal-looking castors on them — and in the fact that when Mr Chidley took the lino up, considerable dry-rot was revealed in the floor-boards. It made no difference. Replacing the lino temporarily, Mr Chidley said he'd best lend us a lighter fireside chair — one with square legs that wouldn't go through the floor so easily, though for safety's sake we'd better use it on the other side of the fire... It was Mrs Thompson's fault. She were a heavy piece and where the floor had given way was where *she'd* always sat in the chair.

She wasn't any heavier than I was. Moreover, there wasn't anywhere else one could situate the chair, in a room that was so small. One Victorian horsehair sofa, one Victorian horsehair armchair, the sideboard, the claw-legged table, two mahogany-backed horsehair dining-chairs — shift one of them an inch from its appointed place and it was like looking at an undone jigsaw.

The fireside chair was smaller, however. It did fit on the opposite side of the hearth. Wedged against the sideboard, admittedly, but it was light enough to move if you wanted to open the sideboard door. It was more with-it looking, too. Its

brown velvet cushions and polished wooden arms gave a certain modernity to a room that otherwise resembled a Victorian railway waiting-room. Alas, modernity wasn't ours for long. As soon as Mr Chidley had repaired the floor — not completely, of course, just an insert of joisting topped with a couple of short lengths of floorboard: no sense in being rash when there was a war on — back came the old chair and off went the new one, to reign in state in the unused parlour we only went through to go to bed.

I was beginning to realise how one-track-minded country people were. It wasn't only Mr Chidley. The Thorntons were having trouble with their landlady, Miss Rice, over her peculiar ideas about moths. Nature study was another of Andrew's hobbies. He kept jam-jars of pondwater on the mantelshelf, so he could look at it through his microscope, and tadpoles in old glass battery cases, so he could watch them turn into frogs. When he caught a poplar hawkmoth earlier in the summer and it laid a batch of eggs which duly hatched out into caterpillars, which he now kept in a fish-tank — on top of Miss Rice's piano, which you remember

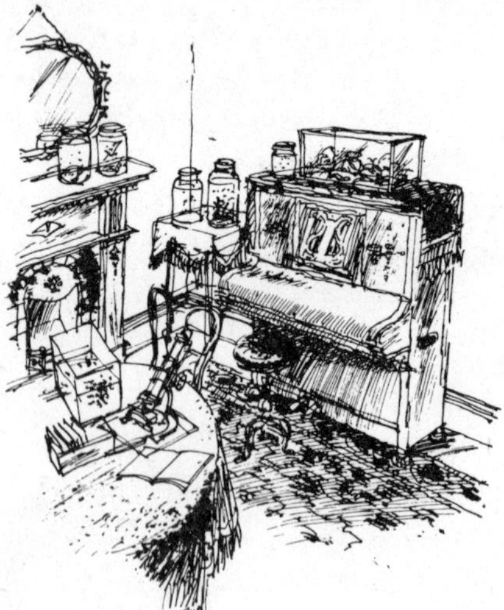

didn't work — so great was his naturalist's enthusiasm that he had to show them to everybody.

It was all right with us. We were most interested to know that the poplar hawk-moth has a three-inch wing-span, and that the hundred or so large horned caterpillars busily stuffing themselves with poplar leaves would one day be moths with three-inch wing-spans too. When they achieved that state, Andrew planned to release them in a poplar tree down by the river to start another hawk-moth colony — his contribution to ecology in a destructive wartime world.

So far as Miss Rice was concerned, however, there was only one kind of moth: the sort that chewed holes in clothes. She hadn't minded the pondwater; if Mr Thornton wanted to catch pondfever, she said, that was up to him. She didn't even mind the tadpoles; she'd kept them herself as a child. But moths with three-inch wing-spans tunnelling into her woollies, chewing holes the size of teaplates in her blankets... There was only one way to combat them: mothballs.

While tanks and troop transports rolled through the village in a constant stream to the coast; while Lancaster and

Wellington bombers roared overhead in their hundreds, darkening the sky like thunderclouds; while what appeared to be a new kind of haystack sprang up along the verges of the country roads leading south — dumps of stores and ammunition covered with camouflage tarpaulins, which nobody ever thought of touching — Miss Rice spent the summer fighting her own private war with the aid of pound upon pound of mothballs.

She didn't say what she was up to, but the smell hit you when you went in like that of a mothball fish-and-chip shop. She couldn't put them in the Thorntons' rooms, but she put them everywhere else. Jane said she'd even found them in the kitchen, ranged around the skirting; she'd wondered whatever they were. When she swept the floor, they rolled about like marbles. It had been no use, either, Andrew explaining to Miss Rice that hawkmoths were really more like butterflies, except that they flew at dusk and by night. Moths he'd said: moths they were. And as for the flying-by-night business, after that, to calm her nerves, he had to keep a cover on the tank in case they hatched out during the night and got up to her bedroom while she was asleep.

How anybody could be so *obtuse*! said Andrew. Jane said how about his own obtuseness in insisting on keeping them? He couldn't *abandon* them, said Andrew, shocked at the thought. He was beginning to think there might be something in being posted to Eastern waters, though; they liked butterflies and things out there; he'd be able to take his hawkmoths with him. Meanwhile Miss Rice went on buying up mothballs in Weston's. I saw her at it once myself, enquiring anxiously when the next consignment would be in since, like everything else, they were scarce.

Another aspect of rural one-track-mindedness I was beginning to discover was that certain perquisites were regarded as inviolable. Regular passengers invariably sat in the same seats on the village bus, for instance. For a start, on the 8.15 to town in the morning, two sisters always sat on the front right-hand seat behind the driver. They didn't come aboard until two villages after ours, and the bus started its journey back at Ashington. It made no difference. Nobody ever sat in that seat until the two sisters got on — and if they happened not to be in sight when we reached their bus-stop, the driver stopped anyway and waited for them. The front seat on the left inside the door was reserved on market days for the wife of a local farmer. Plump, wheezy-breathed, taking chickens and honey to town in a large oval wicker basket, it was the only seat into which she and the basket fitted.

Two seats back, already on the bus when I got on and forever staring morosely out of the window, sat a scruffy individual in ragged old clothes who looked as if he worked at a sewage farm. When you passed by his seat it smelled like it, too. Nobody ever sat by him.

At a safe distance behind him, in a block either side of the aisle, sat a covey of the town high school girls, seniors mostly, in bottle green uniforms and green velour hats with fetchingly manipulated brims. Chattering away in high, bright voices, they were very conscious of being superior young ladies.

Behind them I myself sat, in my appointed place on the left, listening to all that went on. Behind me again, on the long hard back seat, a row of shopgirls, Mr Chidley's granddaughter Marleen among them, swopped accounts of the previous evening's activities. Marleen rarely visited her grandfather and didn't know me, but he'd pointed her out once through the window. Quiet little thing she was, he'd said. Didn't bother a bit about boys. Oh no? He should have sat where I did!

Towards the front of the bus on the right, halfway between the schoolgirls and the sisters, sat a woman who got on the bus when I did. She never spoke, though; just clambered aboard with what I came to think of as her barter of the day and sat staring straight ahead with grim preoccupation.

She worked in a greengrocer's near the Food Office — I'd seen her in there as I passed — and the barter consisted of items she could sell in the shop. Pussy willows in February, blackcurrant bushes in March, bunches of wallflowers in April — they duly appeared in the window later in the day, obviously by arrangement with the proprietor. The look of intense preoccupation was, I decided, the result of the rural habit of scraping together every possible penny — understandable, seeing how poor country people had always been. But when it came to her cornering the local mushroom crop to sell in the greengrocer's — and the rest of the village accepting it — that was an example of rural prerogative up with which I was not prepared to put.

That, however, was a month or two away. Meanwhile I sat fascinated on the bus every morning watching a modern version of the *Canterbury Tales*. I saw the sisters accompanied for a week by a very young sailor, obviously home on leave, and obviously the fiancé of the youngest girl, since they now sat holding hands on the front seat while the older sister sat behind them. The following week the older sister was on the front seat alone. Had the younger one been married? Indeed she had. The week after that she was back with a wedding ring and in due course her coat began to bulge. At last she stopped coming. The older sister, who was plain and very spotty, sat in the front seat alone. Nobody ever joined her.

At the end of the summer term the schoolgirls vanished.

Six weeks later they returned. Four of them now very self-consciously wore grown-up clothes and talked of their office jobs. At the back of the bus Marleen and her friends continued their sagas of romantic adventure. Marleen boasted now about a boyfriend she referred to as Alabam: nót surprisingly, he was from Alabama. One or two of her companions queried Alabam's existence, but he existed right enough. Returning one night from a visit to the pub at Ashington—Andrew, Jane, Charles and myself—Andrew, hearing a movement over a gate and thinking it might be a fox or a badger, shone his torch over it with a naturalist's curiosity. It lit up a G.I. embracing a girl who, with her blonde pageboy hairstyle, her scarlet coat and her black wooden wedge-soled shoes, could have been nobody else but Marleen, even though she did keep her face firmly hidden.

Andrew switched off the torch and we walked swiftly on. I didn't reveal that I knew who she was, but Charles and I, when we got home, in the security of our sitting-room speculated as to where she was supposed to be. Probably improving her knowledge at night-school we decided. Which, said Charles, was more or less what she *had* been doing when you came to think of it, though not in the way her grandfather would have interpreted it.

Now it was July, and the barter woman began to appear with baskets of mushrooms. Mushrooms in summer? I had a word with Mr Chidley. 'I thought they weren't around until September.' 'Ah they be,' he said. 'Specially round here, where the mists do lie on the fields at night. Best time of year to pick 'em — they aint got worms. Nobody bothers about 'em, though, 'cept this Mrs Pottle, and she picks the fields behind the church.'

Mrs Pottle was the barter woman, and apparently I was right about her preoccupation with saving money. When Mr Chidley commented admiringly that *she'd* got a long stocking, he wasn't referring to the length of her legs.

So for a while Charles and I picked the mushrooms in the river fields, sharing our modest spoils with Mr Chidley and Mrs Charleycott, and Mrs Pottle supplied the greengrocer from the fields behind the church and nobody else picked *any*. This mushroom-picking monopoly is a serious affair, as we were to discover when we lived in other villages. In our next one, for instance, the mushrooms grew in the field right opposite the post office and were the prerogative of the village postmistress. A large, brawny woman, she was reputed to sit on a chair outside the post office door watching them come up at five o'clock in the morning. The silly thing was she didn't like mushrooms herself, and when she'd picked them she gave them to the neighbours. Woe betide a neighbour who tried to pick them himself, however. It was the principle of the thing that mattered.

In my early country days at Mr Chidley's, I wasn't aware of the nuances of this. I knew about the pecking order on the bus, of course. But mushrooms, growing wild? If the farmer in whose fields they grew didn't want them himself, surely it was a case of first come, first served? I took to persuading Charles, on our evening strolls, to go along the path through the fields behind the church. It was a pleasant walk, leading in fact across to the river fields, from which there was another path that came out near Mr Chidley's.

There weren't all that many mushrooms in the river fields and if they grew in profusion behind the church — which they obviously did, judging by the size of the basket Mrs Pottle heaved aboard the bus every morning — why, I argued, shouldn't we have some of those as well? At least we didn't want to sell any.

We didn't find a single mushroom in the church fields: obviously Mrs Pottle had already combed them. Just as well too, said Charles, who had visions of her and me doing violent battle with mushroom baskets. But I went that way one Saturday afternoon when Charles was on duty — actually just for the walk. Who on earth would think of finding mushrooms unmolested on a Saturday afternoon?

There they were, though, scattered over the grass as if it had been raining the tops of cream cartons. There is something magical about a growing mushroom. It never actually looks *real*. My mind whizzing as to what had happened — was Mrs Pottle ill? . . . was it that she didn't pick them on Saturdays on account of not going to town till Monday morning — I shot back to Mr Chidley's, grabbed my shopping basket, raced back again to the church fields, and started gathering the mushrooms frantically, filling the basket like a cornucopia.

That I think, looking back, was when I really became a

countrywoman. I suddenly started feeling guilty; looking round to make sure I hadn't been seen. All my resolutions about what I'd say to Mrs Pottle if *she* turned up — they were as much mine as hers; I'd got there first — disappeared down the drain. Better get out fast, I told myself. What on earth would I do if I met her?

I almost did. I was in the second field when conscience struck, having picked all the mushrooms in the first. I was heading back towards the stile when I spotted Mrs Pottle over the hedge, wandering about the first field with her basket. She was staring about her with a look first of amazement, then of chagrin, on her face. Then she started determinedly for the field that I was in. I stood my ground till I saw her hand appear on the stile; then, as she got over, I nipped, coward that I was, through the hole in the hedge — so that we were once more on opposite sides — and crouching as low as I could in its shelter, I crept round to the river fields, up the path that emerged near Mr Chidley's, and quickly along the road and through the door.

He was out. Up at Mrs Charleycott's, no doubt. He usually had tea there on Saturday afternoons. So he didn't see my haul, which was just as well, because when, as was bound to happen, the news got round about somebody poaching Mrs Pottle's prerogative, he'd never have been able to keep quiet about it. That was another thing I'd learned. Countryfolk may be tight as whelks about their own affairs, but they gossip like drains about other people's.

I didn't keep even a plateful of mushrooms for Sunday breakfast, for fear of arousing suspicion. I packed them up in two large boxes — the post office functioned then on Saturday afternoon — and sent one off to my grandmother and the other to Charles's mother. They were gone before Mr Chidley returned. Even so, on

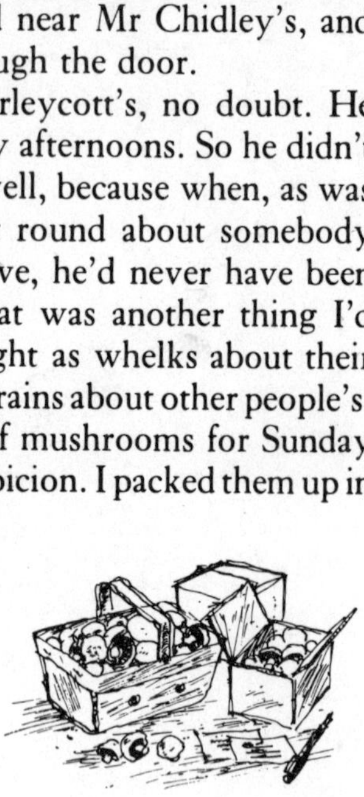

Monday morning, when I saw Mrs Pottle at the bus stop with Sunday's harvest in a basket on her arm, was there suspicion in the look she gave me? I wondered. Did she know it was I who'd had her Saturday mushrooms? *Her* mushrooms, you notice. Rebel I might, but even I accepted the country code in the end.

Chapter Eleven

The winter passed and the war was nearing its end, which was just as well for Mr Chidley's furniture. It was just as well for the patients in one of Bristol's hospitals, too. Louisa, with a sudden upsurge of ambition, had joined the St John Ambulance Brigade and was attending First Aid classes. When she'd passed her exams, she wrote to tell me, she was going to volunteer for part-time nursing in the hospital where, until Charles came back from the Middle East, I had worked with the Red Cross.

I'd seen some pretty awful sights during my time there; experiences I would not want to describe in this book. Louisa dealing with things like that . . . Would she be able to stand it? I had a word with my grandmother the next time we were home on leave. She didn't know about Louisa standing it, said Grandma, it was whether the patients would survive that worried her. Louisa kept roping her in for bandaging practice — roping being the operative word. When Louisa applied slings and triangular bandages for fractured jaws, it was more like being bound and gagged.

When in due course the time arrived for her First Aid exam, according to Louisa's own account even the examining doctor was rendered speechless. It seems that for the practical test the examinees were divided into pairs and Louisa and her friend Eileen — who was as tall as Louisa was short — were shown a man lying on the floor of the examination room and told that he was in the river, drowning, and they were supposed to happen by and go to his rescue. The river bank was shown on the floor by a curving chalk mark, with a pair of parallel chalkmarks a little further on to indicate a wooden bridge.

Action started. Louisa and Eileen came strolling along the imaginary river bank, and the man began to shout and throw up his arms. Louisa and Eileen galloped promptly to the rescue... The doctor groaned. 'You're in the *river*,' he said. 'Can't you see the chalkmarks?'

They took up their correct positions on the imaginary bank. What they were supposed to do was haul him from the river, resuscitate him, summon help, and supervise the construction of a makeshift stretcher to get him across the wooden bridge (a gate lifted off its hinges, I remembered from my own First Aid instruction, or a coat with a couple of sticks from the hedgerow thrust through it as carrying poles).

Apparently what they actually did — overcome by examination nerves and all they had been taught immediately forgotten — was kneel down, put their hands on the man's forehead, and look at each other with concern. Then, while Eileen held one of the man's hands (presumably to comfort him while he drowned), Louisa got up, dashed across the imaginary bridge and, dialling 999 in an imaginary phone box, shouted 'Help! A man's drowning in the river!'

In reply to the doctor's enquiry as to what she thought she was doing,

Louisa said she was summoning help. 'But you're on a river bank!' said the anguished examiner. There was a telephone box on the towpath, Louisa informed him, continuing to hold the imaginary phone to her ear.

'You're in the river again!' was all the doctor could think to say, Louisa having once more put her foot over the chalk mark. She couldn't be, said Louisa firmly. She was in a telephone box.

It sounds incredible, but that was the story as Louisa told it. She could hardly believe it herself in retrospect, she said. My grandmother said matter-of-factly that *she* could. That was just how Louisa *would* have behaved in a situation like that.

Louisa and Eileen passed, nevertheless. When you analysed it the reasoning did have some logic in it, even if it was Louisa's own peculiar brand. The examiner probably didn't want to discourage them completely anyway, said Charles; they'd be better than nothing in an emergency. That, of course, depended. If you were in a river drowning, Eileen holding your hand and Louisa looking for a telephone would be better than nobody around at all. When it came to an otherwise well-run hospital, however, with patients lying in their beds thinking placidly ahead to suppertime, think of the havoc that could be caused by somebody like Louisa absentmindedly administering ice-cold bedpans.

Fortunately it never came to that. The war was over before Louisa completed the subsequent course in Home Nursing which was the other prerequisite of hospital work. She and Eileen marched in their uniforms in the Victory Parade, however, and managed to get in a muddle over that. As instructed, they'd taken their greatcoats in case it rained. (They hadn't worn them for ages, explained Louisa.) They left them in an anteroom during the service in the cathedral, later folding them shipshape and in military fashion over their arms for the march-past through the city, during the course of which it did start to rain and the order came to put their coats on, which the contingent obediently did.

The rule was that the hems of greatcoats had to be fourteen inches from the ground, obviously with parades like this in mind. It ensured that, whether the marchers were short or tall, the length of the legs marching past all looked the same. Except that in this particular squad, naturally on the side nearest the Lord Mayor's dais, there marched two who looked like Revnell and West. A tall one, with her coat hem nearly up to her knees, who had difficulty in swinging her arms, and a short one trudging along in a coat practically down to her ankles, her hands halfway up the sleeves.

You realise what had happened. So did I. But did it occur to Eileen and Louisa? No—and this is absolutely true. Louisa was recalling it only the other day. She decided she must, in an erroneous moment, have bought a coat that was too big; Eileen thought hers must have shrunk. They were standing at a bus-stop after the parade, waiting to come home, when Louisa put her hand into her pocket and found she hadn't any money.

'That's odd,' she said. 'I had some threepenny bits in here but I haven't got them now.' (My grandmother, knowing how forgetful Louisa was, had given them to her for her bus-fare immediately before she came out. Threepence — one-and-a-half new pence, that is — would take you right across the city in those days.) 'That's funny,' said Eileen, feeling in hers. 'I've got a whole lot of them in my pocket.' Only then did it dawn on them that they were wearing each other's coats. Thank heaven the war *was* over, said my grandmother. Louisa as a nurse would have achieved results that Hitler never did: probably blown up the hospital while she was at it.

It is only fair to say that Louisa did, in due course, become a fully-fledged St John Ambulance worker. There was now no call for her services in the hospital, however. Instead she and Eileen engaged in the more usual peacetime duties of first-aiding at theatres and flower shows, distinguishing themselves on one occasion by nearly getting locked in a theatre for the night.

It was an amateur performance of *Wild Violets* and, not surprisingly, towards the end of the evening a member of the audience felt faint. Louisa and Eileen were summoned. They competently administered a glass of water, no doubt feeling like proper nursing sisters, and while the woman's husband went to fetch a car, an attendant discreetly let them and their patient out through a door in the panelling at the back of the dress circle. They wound their way down a stone staircase to a side street where the car was waiting. They saw their patient off, then, flushed with achievement, stood there for a while enjoying the air. The show was almost over and they might as well have gone home except that — wouldn't you have bet on it? — they'd left their greatcoats behind in the dress-circle washroom.

Up the stairs they rustled in their starched grey and white uniforms — to find that the door in the panelling had been locked. Down the stairs they rustled again — to find that the street door had now been locked as well. By rushing up and hammering frantically on the panelling they made themselves heard, but only just in time. Five minutes more, said the manager who let them out, and the staff would have gone and they'd have been there for the night. They might have seen a *ghost*, said Grandma when she heard of it — and it would have served Louisa right.

Poor Louisa. Grandma was a bit hard on her, and in the end her training proved most useful — when Grandma and Great-Uncle William were very old and Louisa cared for them devotedly. But as yet that was years away. Meanwhile the war was over, Charles was out of the Navy — surely now, after all the years of waiting, we could look forward to our cottage in the country?

Not yet awhile we couldn't. My father-in-law had died while Charles was abroad, and for more than two years we stayed with his mother. Sometimes I wondered if the country would still be the same, if ever we got round to living in it. Things were changing everywhere. We resumed our old walks at weekends and on one of the first we visited the village tea-room run by the spinster sisters. They greeted us with joyful recognition. Were we married now? they said. If only they'd had a tin of pineapple for us to celebrate, but alas it was still hard to get. At least we could have our two boiled eggs apiece and fruit cake. See? They hadn't forgotten. It was just like old times — except, they said, sobering suddenly, had we noticed the rash of bungalows going up on the outskirts of the village? In the old glebe field, mourned one of the sisters. They'd cut down the beautiful elms where the rooks had nested. They were supposed to be going to put up fifty.

A builder had bought the field during the war for a song, and now he was making his money on it. People had to apply to the Council for building permits, of course, on account of the shortage of materials, but when they got them they went to the builder and he built them a bungalow on a pint-sized plot, telling them how smart they were to go in for a new place and pointing out all the advantages.

None of them wanted the old cottages. Those were being sold to people from town. The village folks' ambition was a bungalow with plasterboard-partitioned rooms which they filled with Utility furniture and garish curtains. Now they were asking for street lamps outside. Street lamps! said the sisters. It was hardly any time since bullseye battery torches had been considered an innovation. Most of these same young marrieds had gone to concerts in the village hall as children carrying hurricane lamps and had thoroughly enjoyed it.

It was the result of the expanding population, of course. It seemed a pity to build over the countryside like that, but people had to have somewhere to live. Even if the village people hadn't looked on the old cottages as beneath their new standards, there wouldn't have been enough of them to go round.

It was the same in business. Charles and I were back with our old firm, and that was an innovation too. Before the war the female staff left automatically when they married. It would have been like a scene from a Bateman cartoon if one had suggested staying on. But they'd employed married women during the war, and they were extremely short-staffed still. If I liked to come back for a while, they said, since I hadn't a house to look after, it would certainly help them out.

I went back as their statistical librarian, which was another innovation. Before the war that would have been a man's job. I was allowed to write reports which were circulated in the boardroom. The founders of the firm would have whirled in their graves. Other women were coming in, too: economics graduates, personnel experts. There was one elderly woman who'd quietly been the power behind her department for years and had done Trojan work during the war. General opinion was that she ought to have management status, but still she ranked only as a clerk. One of the female economics graduates raised the subject with her management boss, no doubt with her own prospects in mind. Alas, widening their horizons womanfully though they were, they still weren't ready for that one. It so happened that they had a rigidly hierarchical dining system at that time. The directors lunched in a room that would have been a credit to Blenheim Palace; the management—all male—ate in senior and junior dining rooms that would have graced a London club; the staff, too, had senior and junior dining rooms—segregated according to sex, of course—well appointed, with waitress service, but definitely of lowlier estate. Promotion in the firm was marked by parallel promotion in one's dining room—a fact of which everybody was very conscious. To be seen going through the door of the next-up dining room was as important as the increase in salary itself. The economics graduate's boss looked at her as if she'd gone mad when she said Miss Crispin should be on the management. 'Where,' he asked—the only thing he could think to say—'would she eat her *lunch*?'

It was a good firm to work for, and it was doing its best to adjust its outlook, but it was like transplanting a Victorian duchess in the down-to-earth postwar world. Take, for instance, the saga of the office carpets, which couldn't have been bettered by the Marx Brothers.

For forty years, ever since the offices were built, the boardroom corridor had been shut off from the more menial quarters by a pair of majestically impressive swing doors. This side of the doors was imposing enough by normal business standards: parquet floors, lofty ceilings, polished brass knobs on the office doors. Beyond them it was superb. A thick, Persian-style carpet stretched away up the oak-panelled corridor from a point immediately inside the swing doors. Concealed lighting lit the gold-leaf lettering on the doors on either side—the names of the Directors, the Company Secretary, the Deputy Chairman, Chairman, Boardroom—these rooms, too, being carpeted and furnished to luxury standards.

On the more lowly side of the swing doors the senior management had half-panelling and lesser quality carpets: junior management had lesser quality still: senior clerks had mats beneath their desks; ordinary clerks and typists had green linoleum. All ordained according to Almighty edict, thus it would doubtless have continued if it hadn't been for the post-war expansion of business and the increase in personnel, which squeezed the accommodation in the

offices to a hitherto unimaginable point where different ranks actually had to share.

The headaches it caused the Works Department; but they triumphed in the end, though it must have sometimes boggled outside visitors. The economics graduate who'd raised the matter of Miss Crispin, for example; she shared an office with her boss. In the old days he'd have been entitled to a fully carpeted room to himself (third-grade, as he was a junior manager, and definitely not from wall to wall). Sharing with Miss Marjoribanks, what did he get? His desk right in the far corner, for a start, so that she wouldn't get ideas by walking over his carpet to get to her desk, which had, according to the rules, to be on polished, but plain, green lino.

Carpets weren't what they'd been before the war, either. His was a bright Utility orange. As nobody but he was allowed to walk on it, but at the same time it mustn't touch the wall (otherwise it might have looked as if it was a section of wall-to-wall carpeting and give him ideas above himself too), the effect was absolutely rivetting. A large room with what approximated to an orange hearthrug in one corner, the manager and his desk marooned on it as on a raft, and in the diagonally opposite corner (so that people coming in to talk to her shouldn't get the idea they could talk to him), Miss Marjoribanks and her desk on the lino.

This confusion prevailed throughout most of the building. Hitler certainly had much to answer for. Part of the trouble was that the building had been war-damaged, and sections had to be vacated so that they could be repaired in turn. The ultimate happened when it became absolutely necessary to house a rank-and-file office beyond those hallowed swing doors. Only temporarily, and it *was* the Company Secretary's General Office, whose members were considered definitely of the elite.

It made no difference. Up came the carpet and down went the green lino in the allotted office over the weekend before they moved in. What shook those of us who walked those august corridors, however — I sometimes did myself with collections of press reports for the Boardroom — was that the Persian runner had been moved from its forty-year moorings. It now started some twenty-five feet beyond the swing doors, showing a stark grey patch where it had been, with the purpose of making sure it was beyond the new General Office door. It looked most peculiar. Polishing never did remove the mark. It stayed that way for weeks, until the office was able to move back to its normal quarters. Protocol had been satisfied, however. Never could it be said in that firm that a clerk got ideas above himself through walking on the Directors' corridor-carpet.

What has this to do with wanting to live in the country? Only that it made me all the more determined; these were the standards I wanted to get away from. At the same time I could see the funny side of them and they made me realise I wanted to write. But there were funnier things to write about than these. We had experienced some of them at Mr Chidley's. I wanted to live with and write about the combination of humour and down-to-earthness I knew existed in the country. Charles, in his remote office in the Accountants' Department, saw little of the carpet situation, but his dreams lay in the same direction as mine. He just knew that he wanted to paint — and one day to live in the country.

Two years later it became possible for us to move out from town. Not too far out, of course. We had to be near enough to keep an eye on Charles's mother, my grandmother and Great-uncle William and Louisa, and of course to get in every day to the office. Looking for a place just after the war, though, was like looking for a needle in a haystack. It was practically impossible to find one to buy. The reasonable ones were snapped up while we were at our desks in the office; the expensive ones were beyond our means. A building licence would have solved our problems, but there were two snags about that. One was that we didn't really want a new place—though beggars couldn't be choosers; the other was that it could only be used in the district in which you were living when you applied for it, which meant we would have had to build on a site in town. Our only hope seemed to be to find a place to rent while we looked around; but they were even scarcer than places to buy. They were snapped up within hours of an advertisement appearing in the paper and, as we were working during the day, they had always gone when we rang up.

We could only hope for a fairy godmother and one day she appeared, in the shape of an office colleague who shared a cottage with a friend in a village only a few miles out of town. A village, nevertheless, which remained unspoiled because of its position on top of a hill. There was no electricity — not in her part of the village, anyway — which put people off for a start. And it was bleak up there — you could get cut off if it snowed in winter — and the people sounded somewhat odd.

They were always feuding and they had very decided characters. Paula was a genius at describing them. She it was who told me about Mrs Melly, the postmistress who watched the mushrooms grow, who was a great friend of hers. Mr Melly, her husband, was the postman and did his rounds on a bike, pushing it daily — having delivered mail to the cottages on the way down — up the three-mile long, one-in-seven hill.

According to Paula he was a small man, in contrast to his buxom wife, and, possibly on that account, had throughout the years performed feats of endurance that would have put a town postman flat on his back. In his younger days he had twice, for a wager, ridden his bike up the hill with his bag on his back and without getting off. Once he had skidded on the hill in icy weather and landed with his bike in the hedge. He had picked himself up and straightened his handlebars — it wasn't till he got to the bottom that he realised he was bleeding pretty badly and discovered that part of his earlobe was missing. Whereupon, according to Paula, he went back, found the missing piece, and cycled off to the doctor to have it stitched on again.

Paula's landlord and his family sounded like characters out of Dickens. Old Mr Trimble had a wooden leg and had been the village carpenter until he'd inherited his cousin's property, which consisted of a Georgian house, three attached cottages and odd pieces of land here and there. His wife, according to Paula, was a nice little woman, very much dominated by her husband. Their only son, Toddy, was short, always wore a trilby, and accompanied his father as Laurel did Hardy. He was always on the other end of a plank with him, helping him dig drains, or up with him mending the roof. Dig drains? I queried. On the roof, with a wooden leg? It didn't incommode Mr Trimble, said Paula. He could go up a ladder like Dicky Lightning, and actually anchor himself between the tiles with his wooden foot.

The villagers made no concession to his infirmity, either. They hated him like nobody's business. On account, said Paula, of his having come into money and so being better off than they were, and the fact that, living opposite the pub as he did, he was reputed, during the war, to have taken the registration numbers of the cars which parked there regularly at lunchtime, reported them to the police, and got several of the locals into trouble for the misuse of rationed petrol.

On V.E. night — this was one of Paula's favourite stories: she recounted it with glee many a time — the villagers didn't burn Hitler's effigy on the celebration bonfire: they burnt the Trimbles' effigies, father and son, instead. Mr Trimble's was recognisable by its wooden leg, Toddy's by the trilby hat (they didn't like *him*, according to Paula, because he hadn't gone into the Forces). They'd thrown beer mugs at the Trimbles' windows, too, and when Toddy ran to the phone box to call the police, they'd grabbed his trilby, tied a rope round the phone box so he couldn't get out, and tossed his hat, as well, on the fire.

When, then, Paula said a wing of the Trimbles' place was vacant — they lived now in their cousin's big house, while Paula and her friend rented the cottage next door — I said we wouldn't want landlords like that. We wanted a peaceful existence!

Oh, they were all right with their tenants, Paula explained. They only feuded with the other villagers. That had died down anyway, what with the war being over and people getting used to their all owning property. When you knew them, the Trimbles were really quite kind-hearted people. They were very helpful to her and Amy. Why didn't we go up and see them that night? She'd tell them that we were coming.

We did. Later Paula was to admit that there'd been a reason for her intense persuasion. Amy had suggested that perhaps her sister and brother-in-law might like the vacant Trimble wing. Horrified at the thought of having *them* next door — a more thick-headed pair, said Paula, you could never meet — she'd passed the news of the vacancy on to me, praised the Trimbles like anything, and omitted a piece of information that would have put a lot of people off, as we discovered when we went up to see them that evening. It was a pitch-dark night. We found the house as Paula directed, made our way up the balustraded steps with a torch, shone it round to find the bell and lit up a big brass plate. *'A. TRIMBLE & SON'* read the blunt inscription. *'FUNERAL DIRECTORS AND UNDERTAKERS.'*

Chapter Twelve

It wasn't quite as bad as it looked. The Trimbles *had* been the village undertakers — village carpenters usually were — but, they told us when we went inside, they'd more or less retired from it now they'd come into money, save when they were specially asked to oblige. Which, according to Paula when I mentioned it later, they very rarely were. The villagers were mostly extremely healthy on account of the altitude, and very few of those who weren't would have been seen dead with the Trimbles anyway, on account of they disliked them so much.

As for the house, it was beyond our expectations. It needed painting, but so did most places after the war. The roof, said Mrs Trimble, leaked slightly — obviously why the male Trimbles spent so much time up on it — but that didn't affect the part we would be living in: it mostly came through in the hall. The skirtings and doors were a dark chocolate brown, the Jacobean-patterned wallpaper had turned almost the same colour, but when she opened the door of the vacant sitting room, facing us was a magnificent white marble fireplace that could have come out of Grosvenor Square. Magnificent Georgian windows, too. She said they looked out on to a walled garden, though we couldn't see it in the dark. Deep Georgian skirtings, delicate Georgian cornices — she held up an oil-lamp for us to look around. Lack of electricity was one of the drawbacks, but Paula had assured us that that was easily overcome. Paraffin pressure lamps were the answer, she said. She and Amy had them. They gave a wonderful light. We must pop in after we'd seen the rooms; they'd give us a demonstration.

There were two bedrooms in the vacant wing, one with a Georgian powder-closet. A kitchen with a pump for water. (Another of the drawbacks, but Paula assured us that was nothing either; pumping water was very good exercise.) A large bathroom with a big white bath and washbasin and a flush lavatory resplendent in the corner. There were cold taps, but you had to carry up the hot water in kettles, said Mrs Trimble; and the lavatory drained into a cess-pit and sometimes it got blocked. That wasn't to worry us, though; her husband and son always saw to it.

We were supposed to share the bathroom, it being the only one, but Mrs Trimble, who'd obviously taken to us and wanted us as tenants, said they wouldn't use it while we were home. Actually they had a downstairs lavatory next to their kitchen and it was my guess that they didn't use the bath at all, preferring a tin tub in front of the fire. If they had to heat the water in kettles in the kitchen anyway, why carry it up a Georgian staircase just for show? While their part of the house was furnished finely, if somewhat fadedly, with enormous tables, walnut bookcases, plated candlesticks and heavy plush curtains over the doors — obviously from their cousin's time — equally obviously they still weren't really at home in it, having lived most of their lives in a tiny cottage.

How they came to be artisans while their cousin had lived like a squire was a mystery we never solved. Even Paula was at a loss over that one. Perhaps the cousin had been ambitious and had the initiative to carry it out. At any rate, we liked the house and agreed to take the rooms, and went next door to tell Paula and Amy. Their pressure lamps were indeed super, giving a brilliant yellow gas-light far beyond Mr Chidley's wick

types, and Amy didn't seem to mind that we'd scooped the rooms ahead of her sister; probably she hadn't been very serious about it anyway. We returned to town on air. We had a place in the country at last! We planned how we were going to furnish it. It was only till we could buy a permanent place, of course, but it was a start. Our very first home, after all this time... Little did we know then what we were in for.

We moved in. The Trimbles agreed to our painting the woodwork white. They had reservations about our painting the Jacobean wallpaper white as well, but when it was done they agreed it was an improvement. Might even do their own, they said. With a copper and brown carpet on the floor — given to us by Charles's mother: good carpets were almost impossible to obtain new; a pair of hide armchairs; an oak, unfortunately Utility, dining suite, but we certainly couldn't

have afforded period; a print of a country scene by Littlejohn over the mantelpiece, showing a farmhouse scene in autumn, with cows ambling home for milking past a pond—at night, with the pressure lamps hissing, one on the sideboard, one on the table, Charles's mother's copper-coloured velvet curtains drawn, and a fire burning in the white marble fireplace, we wouldn't have changed places with anyone.

True our Georgian bedroom was like an icebox; coal was rationed, and there wasn't enough for bedroom fires, and electric blankets weren't as yet on the market, and we hadn't electricity if they had been. True we cooked by oil and it nearly drove me crazy; we'd bought a new stove with peculiar patent wicks, which allowed the oil to creep up cylinders studded with holes giving, said the handbook, Controllable Heat. There was a lever on the front, marked Low, Medium, High. There was a glass-fronted oven that fitted over one of the burners. At Low you were supposed to be able to cook casseroles; at Medium, joints; at High, the lightest of scones and pastry. Mrs Trimble, admiring it, said what would they think of next? Fancy something like that working on paraffin.

Fancy indeed. What actually happened was that at Low the stove went out while my back was turned, there not being enough oil on the cylinder to support it. At Medium it took hours to brown a sausage. At High, which was the level to which I usually turned it, not having all day to wait for things to cook, it behaved itself while I watched it, burning with a clear blue glow which lapped enthusiastically under the oven or round the kettle, and the moment I departed to the living-room to set the table it went up in sheets of flame and the Trimbles came rushing to the rescue.

This was usually in the morning, while I was getting the breakfast and Charles was upstairs in the bathroom. I think they used to lurk in the hall waiting for it to happen, and for that I can hardly blame them. It was their house after all, and while Charles managed the gadgets easily, for a long time, if I tried to light them, I seemed hellbent on burning the place down.

The pressure lamps, for instance. I used to light them, for convenience, on the broad shelf in the kitchen window while Charles was putting the car away in the garage. The principle was simple. You pumped up the lamp, clamped a methylated spirit torch round its hollow stem and lit it. This vapourised the paraffin in the tube; when the torch died down, you turned a screw which allowed the vapour to reach a mantle. You lit the mantle, removed the torch — and bingo! you had brilliant gaslight which, if the lamp was sufficiently heated, you could even carry outdoors in perfect safety.

If it wasn't sufficiently heated — if you lit it in a draught, for instance, which could happen if the wind was in the direction of the kitchen window; if you turned the screw before the paraffin had properly vapourised — out shot a stream of liquid paraffin at pressure, sending flames leaping up to the ceiling. This was easily controlled. You simply turned the screw the other way, the flames died down, and you then re-lit the heating torch and started all over again. To the uninitiated however, particularly when seen framed in the kitchen window, it looked like a case for the fire brigade.

Charles got used to the sight eventually. He knew I knew how to handle it. Not so the Trimbles, who used to come running with buckets of water and stand by while I tried again. I had similar trouble with a primus stove, which works on much the same principle. In the end I mastered them all. For months, however, the Trimbles hovered anxiously in the background while I cooked or lit the lamps.

They also had a thing about tea-leaves, which they requested I should *not* put down the sink. They blocked the pipes, they said, and then they had to take up the floor-boards — a difficulty I understood. So I used to leave the breakfast tea-leaves in the basin for emptying in the garden in the evening, never having time to do it before I left for the office, and was somewhat disconcerted when I began to find the basin emptied when we got home at night. What had they been doing in *my* kitchen? I wondered. This was something I didn't like. They were anxious about the tea-leaves and they probably thought they were helping, but I preferred to keep my privacy intact. I mentioned it in passing to Paula, who, having a vested interest in our continuing to stay there, raised it tactfully with the Trimbles and forthwith the tea-leaf emptying ceased. Peace reigned in the Trimble household — which was more than could be said for the rest of the village, where they were busy quarrelling for all they were worth.

I have since come to the conclusion it has something to do with the altitude — like living in the Scottish Highlands or the Khyber Pass. People who live high up seem to have an eagle-like quality, with beaked noses and tempers to match. Mr Chidley's village, flat as a pancake on the marshes, was as mild as milk and water compared to this.

For a start, the postman had a feud on with the owner of a local villa. There weren't many of these in the village and this one had been built just before the war, with a shrubbery, front and side entrances, and gravelled driveways to match. A new owner, out from town and not conversant with country ways, had recently put a notice saying Tradesmen on the side gate. Actually it was the quickest way in, and the butcher, the milkman and the boy from the general stores were happy enough to use it. Not so Mr Melly, who was the villa owner's neighbour. Mr Melly, too, had money. His aunt had left him several hundred pounds a little while before and he wasn't going to be treated like that.

He flatly refused to leave the letters anywhere but pushed under the front door. The householder was equally adamant. There was much padlocking of gates and writing to the Postmaster-General before the battle finished, but when the smoke finally cleared away the sign had vanished and Mr Melly, postbag on his back, was still stumping stolidly up the driveway to the front door.

Mrs Melly was daggers drawn at the time with a Mrs Lord, who was the Chairman of the *W.I.* — a position Mrs Melly thought should have been hers, on account of her being postmistress and, as she saw it, boss-woman of the village. Mrs Lord didn't see it that way, being the wife of a prosperous estate agent and a boss-type herself, living in the largest house in the village and having women in to do her work, and she'd added insult to injury one day by asking

Mrs Melly if she would mind keeping quiet during the reading of the minutes. Mrs Melly, who'd been telling her neighbour about her corn, which was giving her socks—'twasn't as if the minutes were important, she said; just that Dolly Parkins, the secretary, blahing on and on about what everybody knew already—had turned red as a beetroot, drawn herself up to prima donna proportions and limped out of the *W.I.* in high dudgeon. Which wouldn't have mattered too much except for the fact of her being the postmistress; after which, when Mrs Lord went into the post office to do business, the pair of them ostentatiously conducted it without looking at each other. It was remarkable, said Paula, who'd seen them at it, how they did it.

An extension of this was that the post office itself was the end one of a block of four small cottages whose back doors opened on to a communal pathway with their respective gardens beyond. Each had a drain outside the back door for disposing of buckets of dirty water and such, but when Mrs Melly was mad about anything she didn't bother about that—just opened the door, swung the bucket, and swished it straight across the pathway at the garden. The only warning, according to her neighbours, was that the door would open, Mrs Melly would be heard saying, 'As sure as I stand *here*, Fred ... ' and as she said '*here*' the water would hurtle across the path, which, as it was a communal one with the entrance at Mrs Melly's end, made going along it somewhat chancy. Particularly after Mrs Lord had been into the post office, when there was an awful lot of 'As sure as I stand *here*, Fred'-ing.

There were countless examples of this eagle-like intractibility. There was the character known as the Snail Man, for instance, who supplemented his old-age pension by collecting snails from people's gardens and selling them to the cockle shop in town. (The local snails were said to be of Roman origin; they were certainly larger than the ordinary variety.) He never asked anybody's permission; just went in and poked in the walls with a long iron hook; neither did he speak if anyone was in the garden, but ignored them as if they didn't exist. This was all very well with the original villagers, who knew him, but when it came to marching as if he owned the place into the gardens of newcomers — the people in the villa, for instance, who'd had the trouble with Mr Melly . . . 'Surely he ought to ask,' I said to Mr Trimble, who was watching happily from his own front garden waiting for the balloon to go up. 'What do he want to do that for?' said Mr Trimble. 'He've bin goin' in there for years.'

At the same time Mr Trimble was hoping the villa owners would object. In this he was disappointed. They happened to be out. But people in that village certainly dug in their heels about their rights, and feuded like Kentucky hill-billies when they thought those right were being invaded. They also — no doubt again on account of the altitude — had a habit of feuding just for the hell of it, as a result of which our end of the village was in a state of permanent war with the section over by the church.

The two sections were a mile apart and ours was much the older, there having been a settlement there in Roman times — hence the snails. The church had been built where it was — on the far edge of the downland — as a landmark for sailors in medieval days. The road from the valley up to the church was more gradual than ours, consequently more houses and cottages had been built around it. The general store, too, was over there. We had the post office, but only because the Mellys had always lived in our part of the village and insisted on running it from there.

The church end had the church hall, naturally, where dances and *W.I.* meetings were held. They also had electricity, which made them feel vastly superior. All the more so because, according to them, our end had been offered it when theirs was installed, just before the war, and while they had cosmopolitanly accepted it, our end, being country bumpkins, had turned it down as too expensive and now couldn't have it at all. Not until they put up an extra transformer, anyway, for which we were very far down the list.

Also, while our side of the village got its drinking water from wells and its water for other purposes from rainwater tanks — the bath and flush lavatories at the Trimbles operated like this, the cold water being pumped up from an underground rainwater tank to a cistern in the roof and gravity-fed down from there — over by the church the drinking water was piped from a spring to a standpipe in the church wall and they merely had to turn a tap to get it.

Feelings ran high at all times, though not now to the same extent as when Mr Trimble had been the full-time village undertaker when, according to Paula, the sexton who lived near the church had refused to dig a grave if Mr Trimble was to do the undertaking, while Mr Trimble equally flatly refused to do the undertaking if the sexton dug the grave.

For a while, if the departed came from the church end, the sexton did the digging and they had to get an undertaker out from town. If the sad occasion originated at our end, then the Trimbles did the digging as well as the undertaking. The situation was straightened out, when it started becoming really inconvenient, by the Vicar putting his foot down, and it finally resolved itself when the Trimbles came into money and more or less retired from business, and an undertaker *did* have to come out from town.

I had this story on hearsay, though I can well believe it. What I do know is true, because it happened while we were there, is that one day a boy who'd been staying with his aunt over by the church was taken ill and the doctor, who lived more civilisedly down in the valley and had long been suspicious of the church spring, had it analysed and it was found to be contaminated.

The villagers were immediately warned on no account to drink the water without first boiling it for several minutes. They took no notice, of course. Generations had sworn by the medicinal properties of that spring. Boil it, indeed. They'd boil the goodness out! In fact their stomachs were so attuned to it they came to no harm themselves. But when our end of the village got hold of the story—it went like wildfire round the Spotted Cow—from that day on the mention of 'carpse water', as our section of the village delightedly referred to it, was more than enough to offset any boasting from the other lot about electricity and village halls.

Chapter Thirteen

We were enjoying every minute of our idyllic country life. Even when a wheel came off the car it didn't get us down.

Charles had sold his sports car when he came home from the Middle East. While he was abroad a man his mother had employed to paint the house had fallen off a ladder and through the garage roof. It was a large garage with lots of space in it but, the way things happened to us, he'd landed right on Charles's car and gone through the canvas hood. 'Wasn't he lucky?' wrote Charles's mother to Charles. 'He came down right in the seat.' He certainly was, but he didn't do the car much good — ruining the hood, smashing the windscreen, and bending the steering wheel. When Charles came home he sold it while it still had four wheels and an engine. When the war was over we'd have a new one, he said; there'd be some super new models on the market.

Unfortunately when they did appear there were waiting lists for them, in some cases for as much as a year, so when we moved to Paula's village and a car became essential, Charles bought a secondhand Morris saloon. It was a really solid car, he assured me. A saloon was far more suitable for country life. We'd

be glad of it when winter came and we had to drive in and out through the snow.

We were indeed, but not for the reason Charles had in mind: of it being warmer inside. It had a large sunshine roof that extended right to the back, with a sunken groove all round it. When winter came and we had difficulty in getting up the hill because the car was sliding about on snow and ice, I was able to stand on the solid rear bumper, hook my fingers into the groove and ride up clinging to the back. This added extra weight and usually got us up, if I could hang on long enough before I slid off. As Charles pointed out, I couldn't have done that if we'd had a sports car with a canvas hood.

The winter was still ahead of us, however. We'd bought the car in the spring. As Charles said, it had been well looked after. The paintwork was like new, the chromium shone, and the engine ran like buttered silk. Unfortunately it had previously led a pampered existence as a town car and country conditions began to get it down. The exhaust fell off. One of the doors developed a sag. The adjustable driving seat no longer adjusted. Whichever slot it was put in, when we went uphill it slid back — which was all right for Charles's six-foot legs but I am five foot four, I was trying to learn to drive which was difficult enough in itself, and when I drove uphill I had to hang on to the steering wheel otherwise I shot back with the seat, the car stopped with a bang, and Charles clasped his head and groaned.

Anyway, we were on our way home one night — fortunately Charles was driving and, most unusually, we were going home via the easier road up to the church — when, as we were proceeding along a flat bit, one of the wheels came off. It rolled along the road ahead of us, giving us quite a shock. There was no way of putting it on again: it had sheared clean off at the hub. So, making a quick decision, we left the car at the side of the road and caught the private enterprise bus which came through a few minutes later.

The bus didn't go via the hill we usually went up. Its owner, Woolly Russet, was a law unto himself, and though there were quite a few cottages on Broad Elm Hill he said he weren't going to ruin his gears on that. Never mind Fred Melly riding his bike up it; if people wanted to live there they could walk. They did. Either down to the valley where they caught the Corporation bus, or panting precipitously up to Lane End, in our part of the village, which Woolly reached by driving across the downs from the church.

His journey ended outside Lane End Cottage, which was occupied by the Mellys' daughter Myrtle, and we got the bus there again next morning. Thanks to Woolly having seen what had happened to our car — he drove nodding his head from side to side like a rotund, cloth-capped mandarin, but for all he appeared to be dreaming of far Cathay he never missed a thing — and our having phoned the garage from the post office, by that time the whole village knew about it. We were greeted with grins from the other passengers, advice as to how we could have fixed the wheel on with a piece of wire (not with a shorn-off hub we couldn't), jovial enquiries as to whether we wanted to buy a good car ... It broke the ice, anyway. From then on we were definitely part of the village. It wasn't like Mr Chidley's, where we had always been outsiders. Possibly it was due to the fact that we'd come to live in the village from choice and weren't just staying in it temporarily. Possibly it was due to my being a friend of Paula, who was very popular. Undoubtedly it was also due to the atmosphere on the bus, which was far different from the one at Mr Chidley's.

That had picked up passengers from several villages who treated each other as strangers. Woolly's bus served only ours. By strict agreement with the Corporation, which had its own bus service as far as the valley, he wasn't allowed to pick up people en route to town, and though the Russet Queen's passengers formed two rival factions, according to the part of the village they came from, each of which kept rigidly to its own section of seats and made inflammatory remarks about the other, somehow it gave the impression of a miniature community. You felt you were in the village the moment you climbed aboard it in town.

We travelled on the Russet Queen for a week when the wheel came off. We used it again when our big end went, causing considerable amusement. We laboured down to the garage in the valley at a snail's pace, clanking at every turn, and when we got on the bus that evening we were met by a chorus of ho-ho-ho's. 'Thought theest joined the firm' was one sally that nearly brought the house down. Being unused ourselves at that time to country wit, it took us a while to work out that the reference was to the Trimbles formerly being undertakers and the speed at which we'd been going along. We got lots of quips about

the Trimbles, which we always pretended not to hear. It was obvious that while the villagers were ready to like us, nobody was prepared to like them.

Travelling on Woolly Russet's bus was decidedly a step-up from travelling on the one at Mr Chidley's. The characters were even odder and, thanks to the stories Paula told me in the office, I recognised many of them at once. The fat woman who got on outside the church in the mornings clutching an angularly bulging sack, for instance, worked as a wreath-maker in the flower-market in town and the sack contained what she euphemistically referred to as 'shapes'. Not, as might be thought, frames she'd made in her spare time at home, ready for fixing flowers on during the day, but used ones she'd retrieved from the churchyard and was taking in to use again.

It seemed that this was regarded as her prerogative, like Mrs Melly's appropriation of the mushrooms, and the villagers not only didn't mind it, they considered it a good idea. Once the flowers had faded, they contended, what earthly use was the frame to anybody but the flower woman, who by using it again could reduce the price to the next customer. Sound enough reasoning, except that she probably didn't — and, what seems to me extraordinary, knowing country people as I do now, nobody seemed to have thought of charging *her* for frames for which *they* had originally paid.

There was also the female of indeterminate age who wore her hair in ringlets, a Tyrolean hat, white socks and ankle-strap shoes. The villagers were used to her and took no notice of her on the bus, but she certainly attracted attention when she got off. She worked in a town sweet-shop, rented a tiny cottage near the church, and was rumoured to have been on the stage.

One day she confirmed this — this was before we moved there — by offering to dance at a village concert. Paula said she would never forget those dances. They were announced on the programme as 'Gathering Sticks' and 'Doves'. In the first she pranced round the stage in a piece of sacking, alternately bent double like a Red Indian, shading her eyes to represent the search, or doing a war dance with a piece of wood to indicate success. In the second she went through much the same antics wrapped in several yards of cheesecloth, except that instead of gathering sticks she stopped now and then to carress an imaginary bird. The climax of the dance came when, with an invisible dove on either hand and a look of rapture on her face, she sank on one knee before the footlights and raised her eyes to the roof. There was silence. Had culture come to the village at last? Paula said she felt quite worried for a moment. Then from the back of the hall a voice shouted 'Mind yer eye, Miss' and she knew that all was well.

There was, in case it sounds as though all the oddities lived over by the church (at our end it was considered that they did), an old man who lived in a cottage further up the road from us and sometimes took a sack of potatoes down to his daughter in the valley. Unfailingly he sat on the back seat. Unfailingly, once we'd passed the church and the bus started its steep descent down to the valley, he would let go of the sack, the top would come open and the potatoes would roll all over the floor. It was a small bus — a twenty-two seater — and a sack of potatoes at large could cause havoc. The church people claimed he did it on purpose. Knowing that village, they were probably right. The outstanding character at our end, however, was Myrtle from Lane End Cottage.

As you may remember, she was the Mellys' daughter, which gave her a pretty good start. She was large, like Mrs Melly — a real Brunhilde — and though she didn't often actually travel on the bus (when she did you couldn't mistake it, because she was in the habit of smoking cigars), she marked the Russet Queen's starting point and was always associated with it.

She lived in the cottage, instead of with her parents, because she'd got married during the war — according to my unflagging informant, Paula, to a sergeant in the Coldstream Guards. He was an absolute match for her in size, said Paula, and it had been something to see them when they were courting, roaming coyly hand-in-hand through the lanes. (You couldn't miss them, she commented: Jack and Jill giant-sized.) Then they got married and things began to alter. They argued when he came home on leave—not surprisingly, seeing that he was Irish and she was a Melly, used to having her own way. Things came to a head when he arrived home one day to find she'd not only been wearing his suits in his absence, but had had his best Donegal trousers altered to fit her and claimed that she was entitled to them. 'All my wordly goods with thee I share,' he'd promised, and she reckoned that included his suits, which he didn't need anyway on account of being in uniform and she was short of clothing coupons.

There was a heck of a row—people stood outside and listened, said Paula. There were cups crashing, saucepans being thrown, language fit to curl your hair. He left next day and never came back, and in due course he and Myrtle were divorced. She stayed on in the cottage because, having attained independence, she didn't want to go back under her parents' rule. She and Mrs Melly didn't get on together too well either, being so much alike. So she lived there with a friend called Daphne and, when we walked down to catch the bus, there she'd be chopping firewood, sawing logs or hammering planks together for a henhouse, wearing a pair of Donegal trousers and patently contented with her lot.

Her most recent claim to fame when we went there was that her mother, who was fond of making preserves and was very particular about cleanliness, had not long before tried to sterilise some bottling jars with a mixture of ammonia and chloride of lime and had nearly asphyxiated herself. She was discovered by Myrtle on her daily filial visit, who, instead of throwing open the windows to disperse the fumes or calling in one of the neighbours, lit a cigar, puffed the smoke in her face, and brought her round like that.

Myrtle was said to be hasty-tempered but I got on with her quite well. I used to chat to her over the wall while we waited for the bus. She mentioned once that she played cricket and when I said I had too, at school, she asked me if I'd play for the village ladies' team the following year. Paula said I didn't know what I was letting myself in for—*she'd* seen the team at practice—but I was very thrilled. Country people are supposed to be standoffish, and yet here was I in next year's cricket team, friends with half the village, just through travelling on Woolly Russet's bus.

The car went well for a while after that. We were into autumn now, with bonfires in the cottage gardens, Mrs Melly keeping watch over the mushrooms, winter activities starting up. There were whist drives: before television shut people into their homes, every village held at least one a week, with players coming from miles around, the village hall packed to overflowing and extra tables on the stage. Dances. Concerts. What Paula aptly termed jungle sales. We went to them all, though to our disappointment we never saw a repeat performance of the Dove Dance.

On through Christmas, with the church bells ringing across the frost-rimed fields for midnight service. New Year's Eve, with more bells and a leaden sky. New Year's Day, with snow and the wind blowing from the North. A week later we were on the bus again.

This time we weren't catching it at Lane End Cottage. After a week of persistent snow and our just managing to get up the hill by my riding on the bumper, there was a heavy fall one day while we were in the office and we got stuck in a drift on our way home. We had spades in the boot and tried to dig the car out, but eventually we had to abandon it. It was there for a fortnight, and our only consolation was that Woolly Russet couldn't get his bus up either. He was operating from the bottom of the hill and his passengers had to walk up and down from there — easy enough, if tiring, for the people by the church, from which there was soon a hard-packed track down the hill, but from Lane End it was a long way round, so we started using a short cut known as Faggus's Lane, which ran down across the fields.

It must have been an old pack horse track. It was far too steep for carts, dropping down in a straight line between neglected hedges, and though it was quick — it got us down to the Russet Queen in ten minutes instead of the half-hour it took by the church road — it had a disadvantage in that there were apt to be snowdrifts between its high, north-facing hedges.

We would walk down from the Trimbles, turn into Faggus's Lane, the end of which was always deceptively trampled — by people presumably taking a look at it and having the sense to turn back — and if it had snowed overnight, nearly always round the corner there'd be a several-feet-deep snowdrift, by which time it was too late to go back and take the church road or we'd miss the bus. There was nothing for it but to go on.

We wore gumboots, but goodness knows why we bothered. Within minutes they would be filled with snow. That would melt, only for more to fall in as we slogged ever onwards and down. We would emerge at the other end looking as if we'd come from the Yukon, head for the waiting bus, and sit the rest of the way to town in soaked gumboots that, now we weren't walking in them, got steadily more and more chilled. At night we did the journey in reverse, trudging up Faggus's Lane by torchlight: two steps up, slip one back, exhausted when we got to the top.

Why didn't we stay in town, as Paula and Amy were doing? Because it was a matter of personal pride that we wouldn't give up. Why didn't we take the longer but drier route round by the church? Because every day Charles, the eternal optimist, was certain Faggus's Lane couldn't possibly be blocked. And though sometimes I wondered if we were bonkers, struggling through snow and ice carrying the groceries when we could have been cosily back in town, when we did get home and lit the lamps and carried them into the sitting-room where the Trimbles would have lit us a roaring fire, and pulled the curtains and had the supper I'd venturously cooked on the oilstove while the snow lay deep outside, we had a tremendously satisfying feeling of independence: we wouldn't have changed places with anybody.

At weekends, as if we hadn't done enough walking through the week, we would go for long tramps in the snow. One Sunday morning, after a really hard frost, we tried going down a lane rather similar to Faggus's, only on the further country side, taking the Trimbles' cocker spaniel, Nosh. This lane, which nobody used—at any rate not in the winter, when it was always deep in mud—was filled with a hedge-high snowdrift that was absolutely untouched. Charles's idea was that it was frozen so hard we'd be able to walk on top of it. Imagine seeing the countryside from that height, he said. We'd take the camera and walk down to the pub, three miles below in the valley. They'd never believe that we'd done it!

They did, because when some three hours later we staggered into the pub, we obviously couldn't have been doing anything else. We were soaked, having several times gone in up to our waists in the snowdrift, which wasn't frozen as hard as Charles expected. We were exhausted, having had to carry Nosh after his first hundred yards on top of the drift. Not only did he keep falling in and having to be hauled out, too, but over the stretches where he didn't —to be fair to Charles there were sections which *did* bear our weight and from which the view was absolutely magnificent — and on which he *was* able to walk, Nosh got his feet clogged up with balls of ice which rattled on his feathered legs like Morris men's bells and stuck in his pads till he couldn't walk. Within minutes of removing them they formed again, so we ended up by carrying him between us all the way to the Black Bear, where he thawed his feet in front of the bar parlour fire while we had hot cider mulled with a poker and the regulars looked at us as if we were mad. 'Best take this poker and a couple of pints with 'ee,' said one wit. 'Theest want 'em afore theest get back up.'

Actually it wouldn't have been so bad — we went via the road on the return journey: no way were we going back up that lane — if Nosh hadn't had an idea. Got his Feet Stuck, he announced after a few minutes' walking, sitting in the middle of the road and looking sorrowful as only a spaniel can. We examined his paws. They were perfectly all right. There was no loose snow on this hill, which had been packed solid by farm tractors and such. We'd have to Carry Him, insisted Nosh, turning up his eyes till we could see the red bits: he could feel Rigor Mortis coming on. So, as we couldn't stay there all day, carry him home we did. Up a one-in-seven hill, taking it in turns, with Nosh enjoying a grandstand view from our arms. He was as frolicsome as a lamb when we got him home, but we were nearly on our knees.

After a fortnight the snow started to melt in the valley and we were able to get the car towed into a farm. We couldn't bring it home, though. The hill was still impassable. At that height it thawed slightly during the day but froze again at night, and the snow still lay deep on the fields. It only needed the North wind to blow and there were drifts again across the road.

Came the day, however, when the Russet Queen made the gradient up to the church — admittedly with most of its passengers pushing. Came the evening, a little while later, when Woolly drove it across the downs to Lane End. The lane had been cleared by snow-plough earlier in the day — the District Council only had one of them then and, Lane End being a small, insignificant hamlet, we'd had to wait our turn for its use.

The track they'd cleared only just took the bus; there were walls of high-piled snow on either hand; but Woolly, triumphant, drove along it at top speed, swaying happily from side to side. As for his passengers, when we arrived at Lane End Cottage, we uncrossed our fingers and cheered.

A few days later we got the car up. The thaw had set in now in earnest. The Trimbles' roof was leaking like the Trevi Fountain, there were buckets and bowls all over the hall, and the Trimbles themselves could be seen up on the tiles busily patching up the holes.

Had we but known it, it was a blessing in disguise. At least it kept them quiet. As it was we waited impatiently for the spring, and when the spring arrived, with primroses in Faggus's Lane where the snowdrifts had been and lambs leaping about like mad in the fields, the Trimbles got a bee in their bonnets and went on the warpath again.

Chapter Fourteen

It was a pity because basically they were kindly people. They lit our fire for us at night. They pushed our car when it wouldn't go. They were fond of animals — the household revolved around Nosh and Mr Trimble was terribly upset when he found a blackbird that had frozen to death in the snow. But it was a hill village where everybody feuded, and the Trimbles feuded more than most.

They'd been pretty quiet since we moved in, working on a bungalow they'd started building before the war but had had to abandon because of the shortage of materials. They'd originally intended it for themselves, but by the time the war was over they'd inherited the big house and preferred it to the bungalow. After finishing it, therefore, they offered to let it to Amy and Paula, whom they held in great esteem — particularly Amy, who was a business executive in town, which was unusual for a woman in those days, and the Trimbles were very conscious of her importance.

She and Paula took the bungalow and duly moved in, the occasion being marked by the Mousehole Male Voice Choir, of which Amy was a patron, arriving by coach to stand on the lawn and sing 'Bless This House' — somewhat optimistically as things turned out, but it made an impression in the village and was decidedly one up to the Trimbles, who stood importantly next to Amy and joined in.

Time passed. The Trimbles seemed to be around the bungalow a lot but they always had danced attention on Amy, doing her errands, cossetting her car, treating her as if she were royalty. They weren't quite so busy as they had been, though; they had time to look around, and they noticed that their old antagonists across the road at the Spotted Cow had increased their trade considerably, what with petrol rationing being easier and more money about and people coming out from town for a drink on the lighter evenings.

Increased custom meant more people going to the public convenience, which was in a corner of the yard in front of the pub and was one of the old-fashioned basic stand-up sort that didn't have a roof. The Trimbles found that from their first-floor front bedroom window they could see the patrons' heads across the road in the gents. They'd probably been able to for years, of course, but not in quite such numbers and it was definitely a new angle to complain about. Complain they did, and the landlord had to build the lavatory wall much higher — which hardly improved the view from the Trimbles' but they didn't worry about a thing like that. What with

the choir and putting one over on the Spotted Cow they were sitting on top of the world.

Not for long, however. Amy and Paula were driving home one evening when their car broke down on the hill. They were given a lift by the landlord of the Spotted Cow, who happened to be coming up behind them. He also offered to tow them to the garage next day and Amy gratefully accepted. Without a second thought, because country folk do these things for one another: it is part of the code of rural living. Except that it had hitherto always been the Trimbles who towed Amy when she broke down and when, on their way to the bungalow to work on the gate, they saw their arch-enemy from the Spotted Cow drive past with Amy in her car behind him, the Trimbles were fit to explode.

A tremendous row followed which rocked the village, as a result of which Paula and Amy moved back to town and the Trimbles, after an interval, offered to let the bungalow to us. We hesitated. We really wanted to buy a cottage, but we hadn't found one yet. Would we, too, have trouble if we rented the bungalow? Paula didn't think so. They'd always been perfectly all right with their tenants before, she said. She partly blamed Amy for what had happened—for encouraging them to think they were her personal major-domos and then accepting the Spotted Cow landlord's lift. The bungalow was empty—why shouldn't we have it? Somebody obviously had to.

We moved in. Before long we had trouble too. What we

hadn't realised was that to the Trimbles the bungalow was like a doll's house. They'd planned it, they'd built it, and in spite of letting it to tenants they still wanted to play with it, having little else to do with their time. When we demurred about this we had trouble. In due course we, too, moved away. Not out of the village — we'd grown fond of it and hoped that in due course we'd find a cottage to buy there. We moved temporarily into part of a farmhouse on the further side of the village, overlooking a pleasant, cow-filled valley, and had peace for the first time in months.

It was a lovely old farmhouse, far older than the Trimbles', with low-ceilinged, oak-beamed rooms. The floors were oak-planked, solid as a galleon's timbers, and the outside walls were so thick they had window-seats two feet deep. Our windows looked out on to a garden, which was unusual for a farmhouse. Generally, apart from a strip in front of the house and the yard around it, every inch of land is given over to production; few farmers have time for gardening.

Farmer Salter did. He was an elderly widower with a prim-looking housekeeper, and his hobby, apart from cricket which he loved, was cultivating what could almost have been a Tudor garden, with flower beds set in velvet turf, a huge magnolia tree on one side against a mellowed brick wall, apple trees in the distance and in between, on the other side, a glorious Albertine hedge. Leading, as you have no doubt guessed, to what could easily have been a Tudor privy.

It was the one fly in the ointment at Downton Farm. We didn't mind having to use oil lamps. We didn't mind having

to use water from a spring — it came from down in the valley and was brought uphill by hydraulic ram. We didn't mind that taking a bath — in a bathroom even bigger than at the Trimbles, with the bath on a dais in the middle of the room, huge, mahogany-cased and looking as if it might have been Cleopatra's, save for the pump-handle at the end — meant carrying the hot water up the stairs and round several corners in tall, old-fashioned brass jugs. We didn't mind any of these drawbacks. They added uniqueness to country life. What we did object to were earth-closets, roses round the door or not.

Unfortunately they were universal in that village, with the exception of the ones at the Trimbles. Basically it was because there was no mains water and people couldn't be bothered to pump; even so, when you asked them what they most looked forward to when modern facilities arrived at the village, without exception they said electricity; flush lavatories were far down the list.

Downton Farm was furnished as befitted a comfortably-off farmer: carved oak furniture, red Turkey carpets, old hunting prints on the cream-washed walls. Occasionally Farmer Salter bought antique pieces at sales: he certainly had admirable taste. Which made it all the more surprising when one went across the lawn, up the path by the Albertine roses — armed with the usual enormous key — and entered something which, for primitiveness, could have come out of the ark. It was spacious, like everything else at the farm. It was spotless: the housekeeper scrubbed it every day. It was spectacular: two big holes side by side and a little one in a box in the corner. Was it somebody's idea of a joke?

It wasn't. It was the only one Charles and I ever saw, but in the old days three-holers, as they were called, were quite common. No doubt because of the large families, and in summer, after drinking spring water, they probably sometimes had to take off pretty fast. Unlike Mr Chidley's, where there was a bucket under the seat, there was an apparently bottomless pit beneath this one with, when the wind blew, a heck of a draught that came up through the holes and nearly lifted you off the seat. Add to the fact that, being a pit, it had a capacity large enough for months... it hardly bears thinking about, but that was how it was. Post-war in the country.

Otherwise it was idyllic. We had the run of the farm, helping to herd the cows and with the hay-making. Charles joined the cricket team which played on Saturday afternoons in the field behind the Post Office. Typical village cricket matches that went on and on till the sun went down behind the elms, with white-flannelled players politely doffing their caps and carrying their bats with dignity when they were out.

It wasn't like that with the ladies' team. We had the field on Wednesday evenings, and while we presented a united front when we played in matches — so united that rival teams quailed at the thought of us and sometimes failed to turn up — behind the scenes on practice nights things were very different. The cricket field, which was a gift from Farmer Salter, was in the Lane End section of the village and the men's team came entirely from there, consisting of farmers, patrons of the Spotted Cow, the local milkman and Charles, the demon bowler. There weren't eleven women cricketers at Lane End, however, so in order to have a team at all Myrtle, our captain, had to make the best of a bad job and co-opt some from over by the church.

There was a girl called Mildred, grand-daughter of the sexton who'd refused to dig the graves for the Trimbles. There was Mildred's friend Sal, whom I'd already met. I'd walked over to the general store by the church to get some bread one Saturday afternoon, and there'd been a wedding on, with cars lined up outside — and for no apparent reason there was a billy goat ambling about in the road with a big white bow round his neck. A sucker for animals even in those days, I tried to catch him in case he got run over. He repaid me by chasing me up the shop-steps, which fortunately were very steep, and there I stood at bay while he, down in the road, kept lowering his horns at me and threatening. Eventually I put my head through the shop door and told them of my predicament. Not a soul came to my rescue. 'That'll be Sal Pearce's,' said the shopkeeper placidly, going on with his serving.

Not until the bells started to peal for the wedding party to come out did Sal Pearce appear on the scene. She was wearing a bright blue dress and hat and had obviously just come from the ceremony. 'He 'ont hurt 'ee,' she said, seizing the goat by the bow and pulling him away. Presumably he was destined to greet the bride and groom and I only hope she was right. What I did notice, as she took him off, was that he was most reluctant to go. He

dug in his hooves and leaned back on them, but to no avail; his owner just took a firmer grip on him and towed him effortlessly down the road in a cloud of dust.

She was a hefty girl was Sal, and when I saw her on the cricket field it was a comfort to know we were on the same side — except that on practice nights we divided into two teams and played against each other, and then sometimes she was on the opposite one. Actually she and Mildred were always perfectly all right with me, presumably because I wasn't a genuine Lane Ender. But those who were had to look out when Mildred bowled, because she aimed at them instead of the wicket, while any Lane Ender who caught Sal out was liable to get a cricket bat hurled at her in fury — until Myrtle, as captain and bigger than either of them, threatened to bang their heads together. All good fun, as Charles said, but it was amazing how the rivalry cropped up in everything.

While we were at Downton Farm the water supply failed one day. When Farmer Salter went to investigate he found that a labourer who worked on another farm, down in the valley, had drowned himself in the hydraulic ram house. It was a tragic happening. Goodness knows what sadness lay behind it. Everybody was very shocked. Except that life and death are accepted more naturally in the country and, after the trauma wore off, the Lane Enders were saying that Harry might have been a bit more considerate than to do himself in in the ram house, mucking up the water, while the Church Enders, remembering the taunts about *their* water supply, though very sorry indeed about Harry, permitted themselves a quiet laugh.

The equalisation didn't last long, however. Over near the church lived a solicitor and his wife who liked sunbathing in the nude in their sunken garden — a pastime considered very avant garde in those days. They thought nobody could see them, but somebody did, and being a village the news got round. Imagine the joy of the Lane Enders when the solicitor tracked down the Peeping Tom and of all people it turned out to be a sanctimonious old man, a pillar of the church, who watched them out of his back bedroom window with binoculars while his front ones were plastered with religious texts.

Speaking of the tragedy in the ram house, an odd coincidence occurred while we were at the farm. I was doing some research for my company at the time — compiling the histories of various subsidiary firms, which meant delving into dusty old deed boxes. In one I found a newspaper dated 1805, kept by some long-dead founding partner because it contained an advertisement offering a reward for the apprehension of a thief who had stolen some of their goods. It also contained an account of the death of Nelson, the news of which had just arrived back in England. It was quite an experience to hold the very paper from which someone had learned the news nearly a century

and a half before. I read the account with great fascination; Nelson's body being brought home on the *Victory*, preserved in brandy; the preparation for the funeral in St Paul's.

I was fascinated, too, by the advertisements — for schools for young ladies, cures for stomach complaints, coy offers under the heading 'Matrimony'. I turned the page, and my eye was caught by an account of two brothers having been arrested for murder in the very village we were living in. They'd killed a neighbour for his money and put his body down a well on their farm. The report didn't give the name of the farm, only that of the village, and it had been almost a hundred and fifty years ago. It was interesting, though. A piece of local history. I told Farmer Salter about it when we got home. Had he ever heard about it? I asked. Did he know which farm it was? He looked at me oddly and said 'Here'.

He was no relation. The brothers had been hung for their crime and the farm had passed into other hands. I made a point of not asking where the well had been. But it made me slightly nervous on winter nights, going up the garden to the privy with a torch. Had the well been in this section of the garden? Did the ghosts of the brothers or their victim walk? Had this — awful thought — been *their* earth closet? Things go on for ever in the country and there would have been no reason to change the site. I scared myself so much I had to get Charles to come up with me and stand outside the door at night. Even then I went in with my eyes shut in case a ghost popped out of one of the holes.

As I was interested in history, Farmer Salter said, he'd tell me something else. About twenty years previously he had on several occasions felt impelled to get out of bed in the early hours of the morning and look out of the window. Each time he'd seen in the moonlight what appeared to be a long, low hearse, pulled by a horse and driven by a man in a top-hat, coming along the road far below, in the valley. It never came up the hill and past the farm. Where the road dipped it vanished, then suddenly it would appear again, going along the fork to the right.

He'd always thought it was a ghostly funeral. Maybe he was right. Maybe it was an ancestor of the Trimbles, busy with some long-forgotten business. Maybe it was an ancestor of Fred Melly's. According to my grandmother, seventy years before, when she was a child, one of the big events of the day in town had been to see the postmen drive out early in the morning with the country mail. For lightness the mail was carried in a long box on wheels with a seat on top for the driver, who would be away all day, and in winter, would often come back covered with snow.

Grandma said it was like something off a Christmas card to see one trotting back in the dusk, perched on the long red box with snow festooning his top-hat like the sauce on a Christmas pudding and the horse's trappings jingling like sleigh-bells. Had a forebear of Fred Melly's been one of those? As Fred Melly prided himself on always getting the mail through — even in the previous terrible winter he'd never missed a day — was his great-grandfather, equally punctilious, still busily doing *his* round?

I never sorted that one out. Our bedroom window looked down on that very road but after that, if it was I who drew the curtains when we went to bed, I always did that, too, with my eyes closed.

Chapter Fifteen

We enjoyed living at the farm, in spite of the fact that I went around so much with my eyes shut. We'd probably have been there longer if it hadn't been for a quirk of fate that led us, one afternoon in April, to go for a walk through a wood some miles away.

Charles liked woods. Probably it was a relic of his Canadian childhood, where there were bears and adventure behind every tree. The nearest thing we could find to that in England was a wood that had a heronry and foxes in it, but we went there quite a lot, watching the great birds silhouetted against the sky like storks, flying in to stand on their nests in the tops of the elm trees, or catching an occasional glimpse of a tawny coat as a fox slipped away into the undergrowth. It was far enough away from the farm to take the car, which we would leave at the bottom of the coombe and walk, and on the way back Charles would stop to get petrol from a solitary pump outside a cottage owned by two elderly sisters.

They reminded us of the two who'd kept the tearooms where we used to have the pineapple chunks. Sisters seem to

abound in country cottages. How these two made anything of an income from a single pump miles from anywhere goodness only knows, but Charles decided we ought to patronise them and as soon as they set eyes on Charles they fell for him, like the other old ladies, and came fluttering out whenever we drove up.

I *thought* that after a while they began to look at him knowingly, as though they'd decided they knew who he was. Charles was continually being mistaken for somebody auspicious and having to insist that he wasn't. Once it was a well-known professor, another time a local solicitor, another time a Police Superintendent. It hit the all-time high, however, when one day, after we hadn't been that way for about three weeks, we stopped at the sisters' cottage and, while one of them hurried to serve us with petrol, the other approached my window and, trembling at her own temerity, said 'Excuse me, but *is* your husband Bill Pegg?'

Bill Pegg was the test pilot of the Brabazon, which was very much in the news at the time as the biggest prototype airliner of the day. It was housed at Filton, not far away, and Charles did look a bit like the photographs in the papers — tall, with an oval face and a beaming grin. I roared with laughter and said he wasn't. Charles said he wasn't too, but she continued to look at him uncertainly. 'We were sure you were,' she said. 'And when you didn't come in for over a fortnight, we decided you must be up.'

The thought of Charles up in the Brabazon, going round and round for three weeks, had me electrified all the way

home. Not nearly as electrified, however, as the sister who came out for her usual chat the following weekend. From her coyness it was obvious she still thought Charles was Bill Pegg — only, as she bent down to the window, for her eyes to alight on what appeared to be my stomach jumping violently up and down under my anorak.

'It's a squirrel,' I reassured her. 'We found him in the woods and he's half-frozen. We're taking him home to look after him.' I don't think she believed that one either. She was still looking after us in a daze as we drove off.

We'd found him lying at the foot of a thirty-foot pine tree, having obviously fallen from the drey at the top. It was April but it was snowing; a freak storm, but it was very cold. I'd suggested that Charles should climb up and put the squirrel back in its nest — it was a baby, probably no more than a week old; if it wasn't looked after it would die. Charles had looked up at the drey, swaying precariously in the snowstorm thirty feet above, and said if I thought he was going to climb up there... We'd better take him home and look after him ourselves, he said; that was what people usually did.

Had we but known it, that was the most momentous decision we ever made: the beginning of the domination of our lives by animals that has lasted ever since. But we didn't know it. I put the squirrel inside my anorak. He was beginning to revive by the time we got to the petrol pump, which was why he was bouncing up and down. We took him home, gave him warm milk from an Apostle teaspoon, which he clutched trustingly with farthing-sized paws, tucked him up in a sweater in a shopping basket for the night, and told each other that raising a squirrel was easy; we'd be able to return him to the wood the following weekend.

Unfortunately the cow's milk was too strong for him and next morning he had diarrhoea. He lay in his basket as if dying — such a pathetic little scrap. To try to save him I took him to the office with me and fed him with brandy, warm water and sugar throughout the day. That did the trick. It cured his upset stomach and, having tasted brandy, Blondin decided to live.

He came with me to the office for a fortnight, growing more rumbustious and squirrel-like every day. Attitudes were certainly changing in that edifice. It would never have been allowed before the war. As it was, colleagues came into my office to see him and hold his teaspoon. They brought bags of nuts which they were disappointed he couldn't eat. Being a baby, he was in fact feeding on a mash of cracker biscuits, warm water and sugar — with, of course, brandy mixed in.

He could have continued going to the office with me indefinitely, but he began to chew things up. Files, chair-backs, desk-edges...and he started practice-climbing up people's legs. However much they knew he was around, it

was understandably traumatic to be lost in a particular problem and suddenly feel a squirrel run up one's legs. So, now that he could feed himself, we left him back at the farm, in a large cage Charles made in our sitting-room. We hated putting him in it, but if we didn't he chewed the furniture, and it was only while we were away. As soon as we got home we let him out, and he'd race round the room flirting his tail in excited greeting, jumping on our heads from the tops of cupboards and sitting on our shoulders while we ate. It was only till he could fend for himself, we told each other. It wouldn't be for very much longer.

Eventually we decided he was old enough. He could climb, crack nuts, leap tremendous distances—he'd even built himself a drey inside a bed-settee we kept for guests, using tea-cloths and paper bags which he'd stolen. We'd grown fond of him in spite of his destructive ways. We didn't want to lose him completely. So instead of taking him back to his native wood we decided to free him at the farm, in the hope that he'd stay around and maybe sometimes come to visit us.

One sunny morning we took him into the garden and put him in the magnolia tree. He sniffed the air, flipped his tail, did an experimental skip, raced to the top of the tree and back again and lay flat out along a branch. We expected to see him make for the taller trees and vanish from sight at any moment—instead of which a rook suddenly flew cawing overhead and Blondin streaked down the magnolia, back to the farmhouse, hid behind the front door, and announced that he wasn't going to leave us Ever.

It was flattering, but it did pose problems. We couldn't leave him loose around the farm; they had a dog and several cats and, indoors, he *would* run about on the floor. We could no longer leave him in his cage in our sitting-room, either; he'd discovered how to chew his way out, and however much Charles reinforced it we'd get home at night to find a hole in the back, a pile of sawdust, and Blondin regarding us triumphantly from the top of a cupboard.

We compromised by leaving him loose in our sitting-room with lots of nuts, but they didn't occupy him for very long. He ate some, stored others in our sheepskin rug and down the sides of armchairs, looked round to see what he could do next... Through that Door, his memory told him, there was a passage and then another door, and then there were Trees. He didn't want to live in them permanently, not being an ordinary squirrel, but climbing them when he fancied would be rather nice. How to get out to them? A room, when you thought about it, was just another cage, and from cages you chewed your way out.

Fortunately there was a step down to our sitting-room and the door bottom was a good eight inches above the floor. Blondin never did work that one out—he kept chewing the oak facing under the doorstep, and Charles tacked a wide strip of aluminium over it, which didn't do much for the room, but prevented the facing from being demolished or Blondin from getting out. For the time being, at any rate... It was obviously time we got a place of our own, where we wouldn't have to worry about what he did. It didn't occur to us for a moment, of course, to find another home for Blondin—in a zoo, for instance, where they didn't go in for irreplaceable old oak skirtings. Blondin was definitely part of the family.

There was still no place for sale in Farmer Salter's village, though, and in any case that was now out. Charles had long ago decided that when we got a place of our own it was going to have proper drainage, even if it was the septic tank variety, and electricity, even if it came from our own plant. No way, he said, was he going to wait outside any more earth-closets, roses round them or not, while I sat inside worrying about ghosts. In the normal way, if we'd bought a cottage in that village, we would have stayed on at the farm until the alterations were done. As it was, now that we had Blondin, we had to find something already modernised as soon as possible, before he turned the farmhouse into a pile of wood chips.

We widened our horizons but it made no difference. Anything suitable was always gone before we could see it. One day, however, I saw an advertisement in a newspaper we didn't usually take for a cottage in a 'secluded sylvan valley'. Fifteen miles from town. Modernised, it said. With large living-room, two bedrooms, kitchen, bathroom, garage, h. & c. and elec. It would be sold, of course, I decided, but I rang the agent to enquire. It hadn't gone, he said. It wasn't everybody's pigeon. It had in fact been on the market for several weeks, and he'd advised the owners to reduce their price if they wanted to sell. They were emigrating to Australia in six weeks. If we were real country-lovers it might suit us, but it needed a reliable car...

Which, of course, we didn't have. We drove straight out from the office that night to see it. It was raining and halfway there the windscreen wiper broke down. Charles fixed it as he had once before with his sports car — with string fixed to the wiper blade, one end through each window, and we pulled it alternately as we drove along. I couldn't say *that* wasn't efficient, said Charles. He wondered why more people didn't think of it.

Fifteen miles out, we took a turning to the left. Goodness, this couldn't be far from where Enna had lived, I said. Along a narrow lane to a pub called the Rose and Crown, another turning to the left. . .past a farm, a huddle of cottages, down a steep winding hill to a wooded valley — and there at the bottom was the cottage we had come to see. A cottage that looked familiar.

I'd never known the name of the hamlet Louisa and I had walked through all those years before with Enna — when we'd crossed the ford and, going up the hill on the other side, I'd looked down on the empty cottages in the valley below and longed so much to live in one. This was the place though. Those cottages were a few hundred yards down the lane — pink-washed now, and obviously made into a single dwelling. The cottage we'd come to look at was the whitewashed one I remembered seeing as we'd crossed the ford. Oddly enough, though we'd never been there together, Charles said he remembered it too. He'd walked past it often with a friend before the war.

The cottage was certainly isolated, which was obviously

why it hadn't been sold. And, there being a snag in every Eden, the electricity supply wasn't mains — it came from a power plant in an outhouse which had to be cranked by hand every night. Well, we'd considered having a power plant if we'd stayed in Farmer Salter's village — and there was a proper bathroom and lavatory. No mains drainage, of course; it worked on the septic tank system, but we'd heard that that was no trouble at all — the chemical balance was achieved by a scientific arrangement of pipes, traps and bacteria and it never, ever, needed emptying. That was a mis-statement if you like. We have been digging up the drains ever since... But we didn't know that at the time.

For the moment there was the cottage, small and homely, set against a background of majestic hills. Most of them were pine-covered — the cottage was on the edge of a Forestry Commission plantation — but at the end of the valley, guarding it like a sentinel, rose a great bare hill with the outlines of an ancient fort on top. Dolbury. The hill I'd loved in my childhood. It had been waiting for me ever since.

Needless to say we bought the cottage. We sealed the bargain immediately, before a surveyor had even looked at it. Whatever he'd said we would have bought it. We were as certain of it as that.

It was six weeks before we could move in — before the previous owners left for Australia — but we went out there as often as we could. Measuring for curtains, looking up at Dolbury, going for anticipatory walks round the countryside. What I hadn't realised, all those years before, was that this was officially part of Enna's village. Detached from it, separated by a walk across a hill, but linked with it for parochial purposes because, when the old calamine miners moved away, there weren't enough people left in our hamlet to have a parson or a parish council of their own.

What this meant didn't dawn on us until one afternoon, just before we moved in, we went for a stroll round Enna's village. She and Tom no longer lived there; they'd moved away long ago to the bungalow they'd wanted on the main road. I remembered many of the other inhabitants, however, and some of them remembered me. Enna's Uncle Walter, for instance, now a widower, still lived in the cottage beyond the church. When I introduced myself to him he told me that he'd taken to going to town again. He didn't walk it now—he was in his seventies; he drove a pony and trap. Still handsome, with his high cheekbones and sidewhiskers, still autocratically disdainful of progress: he'd walked when other people had used buses and carriers' carts, now he confounded the cars with his pony and trap. I wondered whether he was once more visiting Mrs Wilson, but that was something I never found out. I didn't like to ask him and, remembering the affair of the turned-off ham, it didn't seem wise to mention his name to Grandma.

He remembered me, however. When I said we'd bought a cottage in the valley...'Going down to live with *that* lot?' he said incredulously. 'Why dussn't stay civilised and live up here?'

It was like our previous village all over again. Well, of course, this was hill country too. There were the same differences: mains electricity in Enna's village, none down in the valley. We had our own plant, but we soon stopped using that; it was old and it took Charles all night to get it started, by which time it was time to go to bed. We reverted to oil lamps and oil cooking for the next two years till the mains came, and we use them still when the power lines come down in a storm.

We had septic tank drainage and so did our scattered neighbours; the valley cottages, part of the squire's estate, had been sold by auction at the end of the war, mostly to people from town who'd had them renovated and septic drainage installed. In Enna's village the cottages had been occupied by the same families for generations and they saw nothing wrong with the ancestral earth-closets, which caused the valley-dwellers to feel superior to *them*—until the authorities brought main drainage to the top village, decided it was too uneconomic to extend it to the valley, and overnight the position was reversed.

To a man they went in for flush lavatories in Enna's village — quite often simply converting the old earth-closets, which seemed extremely logical to them. If you'd ruminated happily at the end of the garden for fifty years, why should you change the venue just because you could pull a chain? Which was why, a while later, when we'd become interested in local politics and were canvassing in Enna's village one afternoon, one old man led us proudly up his garden path, opened the green painted door at the end of it and, indicating the china pan and iron chain inside, said, 'What do 'ee think of he then? Dr Barbara Moore sat there.'

She did, too. On her famous walk from John O'Groats to Lands End she called at his cottage, asked to spend a penny, and immediate fame had been his. We heard later that he still boasted of it in the Rose and Crown and was thinking of putting a plaque on the door to commemorate it.

Such things loom large in rural minds. Dozens of people, when we first moved in, made it their business to inform us happily over the gate that somebody had 'done hisself in in thy privy — have anybody told 'ee which outhouse it was?' They didn't need to. We could guess. The one with the Albertine rose.

It was a bit unnerving when we first heard it, but it had happened years before, and anyway we now had indoor drainage — which was just as well, said Charles. Otherwise he knew what he'd be doing. Keeping guard with a torch on winter's nights while I sat inside with my eyes shut.

He had to in due course when we were in the Rockies, but that was because of bears, not ghosts, and that was still ahead of us when we moved into the cottage, as was so much else. The pattern of life in yet another village — one to which I had come full circle. History. Intrigue. Peculiar characters — every village has them and we are now considered among the most peculiar, in ours, thanks to a sequence of Siamese cats headed by Sugieh, Solomon and Sheba and a donkey called Annabel — all of them as yet unborn on the day we moved in. We hadn't an inkling of any of it as we drove down the hill to the cottage in a car with a door sagging, its exhaust pipe rattling, and a squirrel in a box on the back seat. We only knew that we had come home.